Prol(

April 19, 1865

By mid-afternoon, the small company of Confederate cavalry, now outlaws, were almost fifty miles southwest of Fort Dodge, heading southwest through the foothills of the Sangre de Cristo Mountains. Lieutenant Jesse Quintana was beginning to relax, feeling relatively safe from pursuit, at least from the Federals.

They had been on the run for fifteen days, since they'd hit the small Kansas town of Elbow. That, Quintana was now convinced, had been a mistake. *Hell, killin' two or three folks is one thing; settin' the church afire, stuffed with townsfolk was... well, not the best idea I ever had. Geeze, them folks could scream, though.*

"Whoa!" Quintana held up his hand and called for the column to stop. They were in a shallow defile, a dry riverbed that paralleled the mountains maybe a hundred feet above the grasslands away to their left. "Quiet! Look. Over there. Redskins, a whole passel of 'em." He reached across his saddle and grabbed his field glasses. There must be at least thirty of 'em, forty, maybe; mostly women an' children by the looks of 'em."

Quintana stared through his glasses, adjusting the focus, but it was hard to see much through the heat haze that hung over the waving ocean of grass. The sun was still high in the cloudless sky.

"Comanche, I think. Here, take a look." Quintana handed the glasses to Sergeant Brown.

"Yessir. Them's Comanches all right.... I count maybe nine bucks; the rest are women an' kids," Sergeant Brown said, handing the glasses back to Quintana.

Quintana nodded. "They're headin' this way, an' it looks they got food, an' we need it." He turned to his men. "Dismount! Take cover. Quietly now. Roarke, Sims, Johnson, take the horses to the rear an' keep 'em quiet."

"I dunno, Lieutenant," Brown said, worriedly shaking his head as he swung himself down from his mount. "Takin' down their womenfolk an' little uns may not be such a good idea. If they are Comanche, they ain't gonna be alone. There'll be a war party followin' not far behind, or maybe even out in front."

Quintana looked hard at him. "You goin' sour on me, Brown? Wettin' yo' britches over a bunch o' savages? So what if there's a war party. How many of 'em can there be? I'll tell ya: it don't matter how many there are. They'll be armed on'y with bows an' arrers an' sharp sticks. With our repeaters, we can pick 'em all off before they knows what hit 'em, before they even gets close enough to loose the first arrer. Goddamnn it, Sergeant, we're vet'ran Confederate cavalry. They're just no-account redskins. Pull yourself together, man."

Brown looked at Quintana sideways, not the least bit convinced. He pulled his sixteen-shot Henry rifle from its scabbard, worked the action, and checked the load. He looked around, found himself a secure spot behind a

Comanche

By

Blair Howard

ISBN **-13: 978-1512194425**

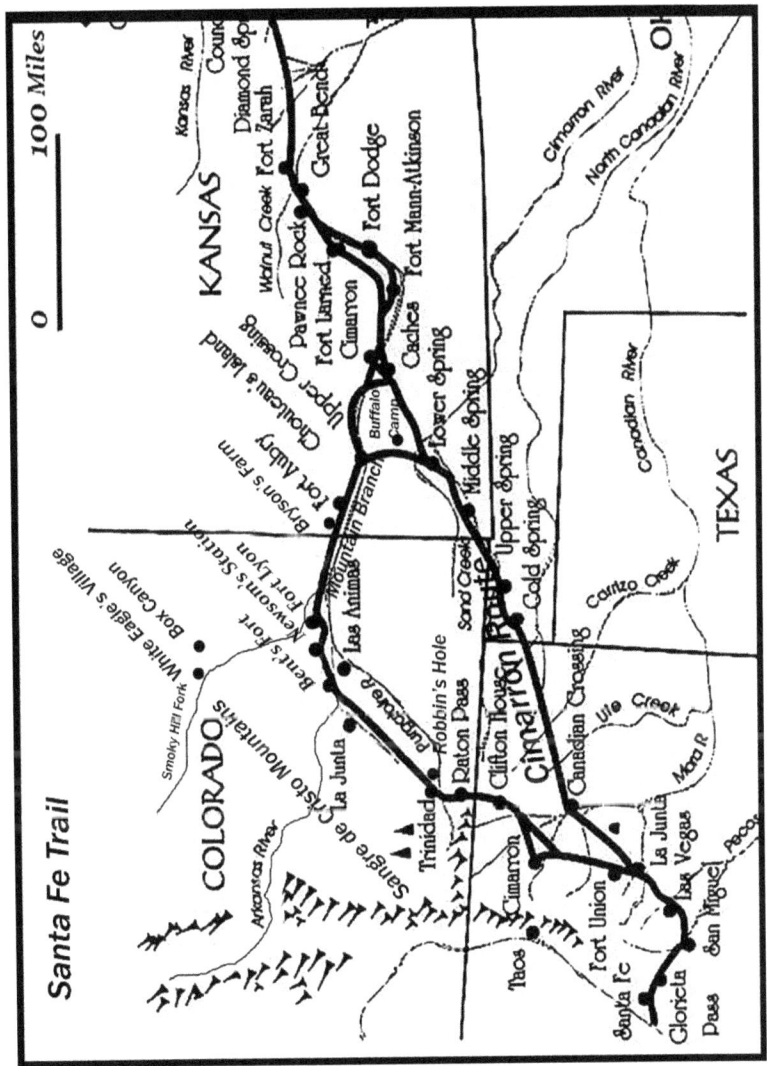

Note About the Map:

I have included the map to help you understand the territory over which the story takes place. Unfortunately, due to the way Kindle formats images, and the type of reader you use, you may find it a little hard to view. That being so, I have uploaded a large version to my website. It is easily readable. You can find it here: http://blairhoward.com/comanche-map.html

Table of Contents

large boulder, and settled down to wait, muttering to himself under his breath. *It ain't the goddamn Injuns that worries me. It's him, Quintana. Hell, he ain't never bin quite the same since his run in with Arch Clement, Christ, that was somethin' else. Stupid bastards almost kilt each other, but what the hell. It's all but over now, the war. All I wanna do is make it to Mexico and spend m'share of the booty.*

The rest of Quintana's men also dismounted and took cover. From their elevated position, they had an uninterrupted view across the vast reaches of the grasslands all the way to the horizon, shimmering in the haze. The air was still, and all was quiet. Even the birds seemed to have stopped singing. As far as the eye could see, nothing was moving, other than the small party of Comanche and the waving grass. Quintana, lying on top of a flat rock, his Henry rifle beside him, his glasses to his eyes, continued to watch the Comanche. Their progress was slow, and he was becoming restless, as were his men. Sergeant Brown was not the only one who doubted the wisdom of what they were about to do.

Still more than a mile away from Quintana's positions, the Comanche were unaware that they were being watched.

Nine warriors rode ponies. The women, fourteen, maybe fifteen of them – it was difficult to tell because of the distance – walked beside travois. The children, some eight or nine boys and girls of varying ages, were also on foot.

Their leader, a minor chief, perhaps thirty years old, wore a headdress made from the skin of a buffalo head and neck with its horns still attached. Under his right armpit, he carried a war lance. Across his back hung a bow and a quiver of arrows. He was a formidable-looking warrior.

The rest of the Comanche men were younger, late teens to early twenties. Their faces were painted a variety of colors. All were bare chested and armed with bows and lances.

The women, aged from fourteen to about thirty, were covered from head to toe in flowing shirts and skirts. The boy children were naked but for breach cloths; the girls were covered with cloth shirts and skirts.

Thirty minutes passed before Quintana was able to see exactly what he was up against, and another thirty before they came into range.

"Not a firearm among 'em," he muttered to himself, a satisfied grin on his face. "Hold your fire, boys, 'till I give the word."

Lying flat on his belly on top of the flat rock, he waited. The stock of the Henry rifle pressed against his right cheek, and the finger of his right hand caressed the trigger. His left eye closed as he sighted the weapon on the Comanche chief. He waited, and he waited, then.... BAM! The rifle slammed back into his shoulder.

The Comanche pitched backward out of the saddle. The rest of the party were taken completely by surprise.

"NOW!" Quintana yelled, jacking another cartridge into the chamber.

The other seventeen rifles fired together, and the rest of the braves fell. So did four of the women. The ponies panicked and scattered, running off in all directions. Three of the horses pulling the travois reared, and then bolted across the grasslands, dragging their loads behind them. Blankets, baskets, and items of food scattered in their wakes. The rest of the party stood still, bewildered, frightened.

"Well now," Quintana said, rising to his feet. "That was easy. Let's go see what we have."

They dropped down from the ridge and into the defile, running for the gap in the rocks and onto the narrow trail that led down onto the plain below.

On the prairie, a young Comanche boy, perhaps thirteen years old, was down on one knee, both of his hands on the ground in front of him. He looked wildly around and saw the gun smoke rising from the ridge above the defile. Seeing nothing moving, he made up his mind. He jumped to his feet and ran to one of the ponies. The frightened beast stood, head down, its ears flattened. Without slowing, and with a mighty leap, the boy was up on the pony's back. With a kick of his heels, they were streaking away at full gallop. He only just made it.

CRACK. Wheeee. The ball flew past the boy's head, and was quickly followed by another, and another. But he was now flat on the pony's back, his face clamped to the left side of its neck, and moving fast, too fast. The gap between him and Quintana's men widened with every stride. He was safe, almost out of sight, beyond range of the Confederate rifles and galloping hard.

"*Goddamn it!*" Quintana's face purpled with rage. "Goddamn it. Leave the goddamn ponies. Grab those horses. We needs 'em. See what's on those, those... cart things, whatever they are. We need food, FOOD."

For a long moment he stood gazing after the diminishing cloud of dust, his rifle resting on his shoulder: *Damn, damn, damn, damn.* He shook his head, and then he turned his attention to his men and the captives.

The women and children had been herded together into a group. His men rifled through the goods and chattels on the travois, flinging whatever they considered to be of no use to one side. They stacked hide-bound packages of dried meat, and other foodstuffs they were not readily able to identify, into piles ready to be loaded onto horseback. There wasn't much. The pile of usable food was pitifully small, but *better than nothing.*

Still fuming over the escape of the Comanche youngster, Quintana turned his attention to the group of Indians now seated, huddled together on the ground.

"Stinkin' savages," he growled, walking slowly around the group. "You, stand up." He pointed at a young girl, perhaps fourteen years of age, maybe younger.

She looked up at him, terrified, unable to understand what he said,

"I SAID... STAND UP." He grabbed her by the hair, pulling her roughly to her feet, and dragged her out of the group.

She stood still, trembling, head down, hands clasped together in front of her. Quintana walked slowly around her, appraising.

"This one's not so bad. Stinks a bit, but not so bad." He looked sideways and grinned at the rest of his men, who were standing over the group, rifles in hand. "Let's see what we got heah."

He laid his rifle on the ground, reached out with both hands, and grasped the edges of the cloth shirt on either side of her neck. In one single downward swoop, he tore it completely from her body, leaving her standing naked to the waist. Her hands flew to her tiny, barely formed breasts in a vain effort to cover them.

Quintana slapped her face, hard, and smacked her hands away from her chest. When he saw the small buds, his mouth went dry. He licked his lips and stared at her, wide eyed. She whimpered with terror.

He took a step closer, grasped the waist of her skirt and ripped it from her. She screamed. He slapped her again. She sobbed quietly as he looked her up and down.

She was still a child.

"Go get the horses, an' bring mine with ya," Quintana snapped. "Let's get this finished and get outa heah."

He looked around at the devastation he'd wrought. The dead chief laid crumpled on the ground some fifty yards away. He walked over to him, taking his knife from its sheath as he went.

"Well, now. Ain't you the han'some one." He looked down at the painted face. "What's all that mess for anyway?" He waited for an answer, but received none.

"Nothin' to say fo' yourself, huh?" *Wouldn't unnerstand y'all anyhow; goddamn savage.* He crouched down beside the dead Indian and grabbed one of the buffalo horns, dragging the headdress off. *There it is.* He grasped the braided forelock and pulled hard, lifting the Indian's head off the ground. He placed the edge of the knife at the base of the forelock where it joined the scalp, and then, with several swift cuts, sliced away a strip of hair from the front to the back of the skull, leaving the bloody bone exposed. Then he wiped the blade of the knife on the Indian's leather vest, stood, returned the knife to its sheath, and stuffed the bloody lock of hair under his belt, next to that of the girl he'd so recently violated.

The sun was going down over the mountains and Quintana and his men were long gone when the band of Comanche warriors arrived at the scene of the massacre.

8

They were led by White Eagle, an older man and principle chief. He dismounted and stood silently, looking down at his son, the leader of the slain Indians. For a long moment, he remained there, motionless, silent, his face somber. Then he turned to face the setting sun. He stood rigidly erect, his feet spread, his arms wide apart over his head, and his fists tightly clenched. Then he threw back his head and howled, a long, mournful wail that echoed across the plain and reverberated around the peaks and bluffs of the foothills.

They gathered the bodies - his son, his son's woman and their girl child, his granddaughter, and all of the others, thirty-eight in all. They loaded them gently onto the travois, those that hadn't been destroyed. Some they had to lay over the backs of the few ponies they had been able to recover. Slowly, sadly, they headed back to their village beyond the foothills, among the mountains to the northwest.

By nightfall the next day, they were home, and the bodies of the dead were already being prepared for their final journey, to the home of the Great Spirit.

That night, the great campfires blazed through the night, casting stark, flickering shadows over the sides of the teepees. The steady, throbbing beat of the war drums echoed over the mountains. The warriors, their faces streaked with black war paint, danced around the fires and chanted the songs of war. Their chief, White Eagle, and the rest of the tribal elders watched....

Chapter 1

Colonel Hiram Richard, the commanding officer of Fort Scott, looked at the clock on the wall and then at Corporal Smith. It was exactly nine o'clock.

"Show them in, Corporal," he said, straightening some papers on his desk.

The two men stepped quickly into Richard's office, stood to attention in front of his desk, and saluted.

"At ease, Captain, Sergeant Major," Richard said, half rising from his seat, then sitting down again. "You're almost a week early. Not bad news, I hope. What can I do for you?"

"Well, Colonel. We talked it over, so we did, the sergeant major an' me, an' we decided to take you up on your offer; we'd like to stay in the army, sir."

Richard again rose to his feet. This time, he walked around his desk, grabbed Captain Ignatius O'Sullivan's hand, shook it enthusiastically, and then turned to Sergeant Major Boone Coffin and did the same.

"Congratulations, both of you. Captain O'Sullivan," he said, grinning widely, "your rank in the regular army is effective immediately, and I cannot tell you how delighted I am that you've made this decision. I had feared after our last meeting that you would decide to retire, both of you." He opened the door of a small

10

cupboard and withdrew a bottle of scotch whiskey and three glasses.

"I know it's too early for strong drink, but this calls for a celebration." He poured three good measures and handed one to each of them. "Pull up those two chairs. Sit! Sit! Cigars, gentlemen?" He walked back around his desk and pulled open one of the lower drawers.

O'Sullivan was about to refuse, but then thought better of it. After all, he did not want to offend his new commanding officer.

For several moments, the three men sat, quietly enjoying what O'Sullivan knew to be the very best of cigars and some very fine drink. The air in the room was soon filled with clouds of aromatic smoke.

"I have already been in contact with General Sherman," Richard began. "It seems he anticipated your decision and has ordered you both to Fort Larned. What he has in mind for you there, I have no idea. The area is, without doubt, a hotbed of Indian activity, some of which, I fancy, can be directly attributed to your past activities."

"Sir?" O'Sullivan asked.

"You will, I'm sure, remember the incident south of Fort Dodge?"

"You mean the massacre of the Comanche?" O'Sullivan asked. "Of course, Colonel. There was a second one up in the mountains some sixty miles farther south. That was something I'll never forget, never."

"I didn't hear about a second massacre," Richard said. "Tell me."

"Well, I have no idea if you could call it a massacre or not. If you count ponies, it was, but how many Comanche were killed, I can't say. Some, for sure. The bodies had all been removed by the time we got there. It was their ponies we found, what was left of 'em. He killed 'em all. We figured Quintana had had enough of being chased by the Indians an' so went on the offensive. He tracked them down at night, took 'em by surprise, killed some – there was dried blood everywhere – but his idea was to kill all of their mounts, and he did. No horses, no pursuit. We found the remains of more than forty dead ponies, all still tethered, shot down where they stood. They'd been rottin' for four days by the time we found 'em. The stink... you could cut it with a knife. Anyway, it must have worked. We didn't see a Comanche all the way to the Mexican border."

"Well, be that as it may," Richard said, "it seems that their leader, White Eagle, is out for revenge. He has been raiding travelers and settlements along both routes of the Santa Fe Trail, and no one can find him. He's constantly on the move. So, Captain, Fort Larned it is. Do you have any thoughts?"

"I'm sure I will, sir, but for now, at least, I can't think what they might be. When do we leave?"

"Not for a day or two. You're back here five days earlier than expected. I will communicate with General Sherman as to the logistics, but I suggest you make

12

yourselves ready travel by the..." he turned and looked at the wall calendar, "seventeenth. Stagecoaches leave here for Santa Fe every week, on Tuesdays and Thursdays. You'll join the escort of one of those, probably the next one, but that remains to be seen. In the meantime, as soon as I know something, I'll send for you. As for now, I suggest you report to the quartermaster and draw your gear and horses."

"One more thing, Colonel," O'Sullivan said.

"Of course. What is it?"

"Lieutenant Warwick, sir. I'd like to take him along, if that would be possible."

"I thought you and he didn't get along," Richard said, with a slight smile.

"Ah well, there you go, sir. We soon brought him around, so we did. He's a good lad. He'll make a fine officer, one day."

"Well, I'll see what the general has to say. If he agrees, we'll make it happen. It will do the lad good to get him out of here. Have you talked to him since your return?"

"No, sir. I thought I'd wait 'till I knew what we were about."

"Well, now would be as good a good a time as any...CORPORAL SMITH!"

The corporal stuck his head in the door.

"Go find Lieutenant Warwick and have him report here, to Captain O'Sullivan."

The corporal disappeared.

"He's not far away, I'm, sure. You can use Captain Johnson's office. I just down the hall, to the right. I'll talk to you soon, Captain; very soon."

Born and raised in County Cork in Ireland, Captain Ignatius Ronan O'Sullivan was a tall, heavy-set man, a little more than six feet one tall, and 240 pounds of solid muscle. At forty-two years old, he considered himself to be still in his prime. His black hair showed not a hint of gray; he wore it long, just to the collar. His facial hair was limited to a huge mustache that swept away from his upper lip to join with even bigger sideburns – a style made famous by Federal Major General Burnside. His chin was clean-shaven, and his skin was heavily lined and deeply tanned. His eyes were deep blue, with tiny lines radiating away from the corners, giving him the look of a man who laughed a lot, which he did; it was part of his Irish make up. He was an impressive man, by any standards, and with a demeanor to match. He stood rigidly erect, his chest a great barrel, his arms knotted with muscles. He had been just twenty-two years old when he and his baby sister, Bonnie, had stepped off the boat from Ireland in 1843. His best and only real friend in the world was Sergeant Major Boone Coffin.

Coffin was a small man, just five feet eight inches tall, skinny to a fault and weighed less than 130 pounds. He was twenty-eight years old, origins unknown, even to him. He wore his thin, receding hair shoulder-length.

His thin face was deeply tanned and clean-shaven, his eyes hazel and hooded. His looks were deceptive. Coffin was an extremely intelligent man, resourceful, and a survivor of the first order. And now, as a "Top Soldier" he had come into his own. He was respected by officers and enlisted men alike. The two men had been together since the outbreak of the Civil War, and they relied upon each other completely.

"So, Ronan," Coffin said, as they sat together in Captain Johnson's empty office. "It begins again. I must say, I'm glad to be back where we belong. I've hardly known what to do with myself these last eight days."

"Well, that will soon change, Boone. What are you going to about that mule of yours? Will you take her with you?"

"No, I don't think so. She's not as young as she once was, and, well, it's about time she took it easy. It's been a long two years for her. I thought I might leave her with Bonnie."

"Good idea. She'll be pleased to look after her, so she will."

"What about Lightning? Will you be taking him with you?" Coffin was referring to O'Sullivan's stallion. Coffin had procured the big horse for O'Sullivan for their jaunt into Northern Alabama with Colonel Streight's mule solders. O'Sullivan had, in return, supplied Coffin with the mule, now called Phoebe and due to be retired. The two animals had carried them for several thousands of miles over the preceding two years.

O'Sullivan heaved a big sigh, then said, "Much as I hate to leave him behind, I think he will be better off with Bonnie an' your mule. They would not like to be parted."

"Her name is Phoebe, Cap. You never once in the past two years called her by her name. I've often wondered why."

"Ha, you'll laugh if I tell you."

"Go on."

"When I was back in Ireland, we all lived on a farm out in the country. It was a bit of a wild spot, where we lived, but not so far away from civilization as you might think, if you saw it. Anyway, less than a mile away from where we lived, on the edge of a small wood, in a broken down old ruin of a cottage, lived an old woman. Us kids swore she was a witch, so we did; her name was–"

"Phoebe? I get it." Coffin laughed. "So you think my poor old mule is a witch?"

"Nah, course not...." A quiet knock sounded on the office door. "Come in."

Second Lieutenant Dilman Warwick was one of those good-looking young officers who never seem to have trouble making their way through life. He had graduated from West Point in 1864, twentieth in his class of forty-two. He was twenty-three years old, a little over six feet tall, with wavy brown hair cut just above the collar of his uniform jacket. His face was thin with wide-set hazel eyes, and clean-shaven except for a small mustache. He kept his boots polished to high gloss and, except when he was on parade, he wore his shell jacket with the top two buttons undone. He was well-spoken, fit and, to O'Sullivan's mind, he looked disgustingly healthy. He came from a well-respected, upper-class Philadelphia family and was accustomed to all of the privileges that came with it. And, at first, he and O'Sullivan had not seen eye-to-eye. He didn't get along with Coffin either, or his mule, Phoebe. Now, however, after many long months together chasing outlaws through New Mexico and Texas, things were different, a lot different.

"Mr. Warwick. Welcome, and good to see you," O'Sullivan said, jumping to his feet and sticking out his hand. "How's the leg?" He was referring to the wound that Warwick had received at the hands of Jesse Quintana.

"Good as ever was, Captain. Thanks to the sergeant major. Good to see you, Boone," Warwick said.

"You, too, Lieutenant." Coffin rose to his feet, taking Warwick's hand and grasping it firmly. He was also smiling, partly because he was glad to see the young man and partly because of Warwick's use of his first name. *My how things do change.*

"Sit down, son," O'Sullivan said, dragging up a chair for him. "We need to talk."

"You're going to stay, right?" Warwick smiled as he said it. "And you want me to join you."

"Hah, ain't you the one, though?" O'Sullivan laughed. "But yes, that's about the size of–"

"Done," Warwick said, interrupting him. "And I'm honored that you'd want me with you, sir."

O'Sullivan was taken aback. "Now hold on, Lieutenant. You have no idea what you're lettin' yourself in for."

"It makes no difference, Captain. I have to serve somewhere and it's better... well, it's better to serve with someone you know. I know I was difficult to get along with, sometimes–"

"All the bloody time," O'Sullivan growled, interrupting him, "and you were about to say 'better the divil you know,' now weren't you?"

"That I was, Captain. But devil or not, I can't think of anyone I'd rather ride alongside than you, sir."

"And it's glad we'll be to have you, will we not, Sergeant Major?"

Coffin nodded, smiling.

"So it's the three bloody musketeers, then," O'Sullivan said, laughing. "Good to have you, me boy, that is if General Sherman agrees to let you go. I'll let Colonel Richard know of your decision, and he'll make the necessary communications with the good general. Assuming all goes to plan, we'll meet at the quartermaster's office at two o'clock this afternoon. Oh, an' you'll be please to know that the sergeant major's mule will be staying here."

Warwick looked crestfallen. "But why?"

Coffin smiled at him. The young lieutenant had at the start of their last, foray, urged him to get rid of Phoebe, but since then....

"She's gettin' too old, Dil," Coffin said. "It's time she took it a bit easy. She'll stay in Elbow, with Bonnie, along with the captain's horse. They'll grow old together."

The lieutenant nodded. "Two o'clock, then." He stood, saluted O'Sullivan, spun on his heel, and walked quickly from the room.

"You know, Boone," O'Sullivan said, thoughtfully. "I do believe the boy had a tear in his eye."

Chapter 2

Fort Larned, Kansas, July 25

The bi-weekly Overland Mail coach left Fort Scott at seven o'clock on Tuesday morning, July 18th. The coach carried four passengers and several boxes of sundry items, including letters and parcels and was escorted by a small detachment of eight troopers and a sergeant. O'Sullivan, Coffin and Warwick tagged along with the escort, much to the escort sergeant's discomfort.

It was a little more than three hundred miles from Fort Scott to Fort Larned via Emporia, where they would join the Santa Fe Trail and another, larger coach.

They arrived in Emporia two days later at six o'clock on the afternoon of the twentieth and stayed overnight at a hotel next to the livery stable. They left at six o'clock the following morning and continued southwest along the Santa Fe Trail, arriving at Fort Larned a little after seven o'clock on the evening of the twenty-fourth.

Tired as they all were, O'Sullivan felt that he should report immediately to the commanding officer, Lieutenant Colonel Jesse Leavenworth.

He dismounted, wearily, handing the reins of his horse to Coffin. "I need to report in. Boone, have someone take care of the horses, then go see if you can find us something to eat. We'll join you as soon as we can. Dil, you come with me."

Together, they walked over to the command office, where they were greeted by the duty sergeant.

"Good evening, Captain." Sergeant Walker rose from his seat. "It's good to see you again, sir. You, too, Lieutenant. Yes, Colonel Leavenworth is still here. If you'd like to sit." He indicated a row of chairs set against the wall. "I'll let him know you're here." Walker walked to the rear of the office, knocked on the door, opened it, and said something that O'Sullivan was unable to hear.

"He'll be just a moment, Captain."

The inner office door opened almost immediately and a large, jovial man dressed in the uniform of a Lieutenant Colonel appeared. He smiled broadly.

Jesse Leavenworth was a little overweight with a large round face topped by a bald and shiny pate. He sported a set of whiskers that rivalled O'Sullivan's own.

"Good evening to you, Captain, Lieutenant," he boomed. "I've been expecting you. It's good to see you again. Come on in. I was just about to leave; go home, get something to eat, but never mind...." He glanced up at the clock on the wall.

"Colonel Leavenworth, sir," O'Sullivan said. "We didn't mean to interrupt you at this hour. I just wanted to let you know that we're here. We can talk in the morning, if you prefer."

"Capital thought, Captain, capital thought. Let's do that. We have much to discuss, and I'm sure you must be tired. Nine o'clock shall we say, then? Good, good. SERGEANT WALKER!" he shouted.

"Yes, Colonel," Walker said, poking his head around the door.

"You have accommodations for these gentlemen, correct?"

I do, Colonel."

"Well, then. There it is. You two go and get settled in, have something hot to eat. Walker, tell the mess sergeant I said he is to prepare a meal for the captain, the lieutenant and the sergeant major... he is with you, yes?"

"He is, sir. He's seeing to the horses and our gear."

"Good. See you in the morning, then. Nine o'clock sharp."

"I assume you know why you're here?" A little after nine 'clock the next morning. O'Sullivan and Colonel Leavenworth were seated together in the colonel's office, drinking scalding black coffee.

"Not so much, sir. Colonel Richard said something about that incident out on the trail, the massacre of a band of Comanche. That's about it."

"Well, Captain, that's not all there is to it. We have no idea how many Comanche were killed that day, but it must have been thirty or forty. They were a part of a breakaway group of more than three hundred Kwahadi Comanche, including the women and children. They are led by a chief by the name of White Eagle.

"White Eagle's son, his son's wife, and his granddaughter were all among the slain. Bad business, very bad business. Needless to say, the chief is out for revenge. He's been raiding settlements, way stations and outposts along both branches of the Santa Fe ever since. Why, he even hit Fort Dodge last month. It was after dark, so there were no casualties, but he did get away with more than thirty horses."

O'Sullivan nodded, "Tell me about this White Eagle, Colonel."

"There's not much to tell. We know little about him. We do know that he and his group separated from the main band some five, six, years ago and then disappeared into the mountains. We don't where, and we don't know exactly how many, but there must be at least 150 of them. Warriors, that is, and at least that many more women and children.

"The Kwahadi are the most warlike of the Comanche nation. They are horse thieves, cattle thieves, masters of guerilla tactics. They will not stand and fight. Instead, they prefer to use stealth and surprise. They hit hard and fast and then they run.

"They hate the white man in general, Mexicans in particular, and blacks almost as much. What Quintana did only made a bad situation worse. White Eagle, though, seems to be a law unto himself and owes allegiance to no one other than himself and his own people.

Leavenworth paused, looked at the clock on the wall, the continued, "And one more thing, Captain. Contrary to popular belief, the Comanche *will* attack at night, mostly during a full moon, but not always, and when they think the enemy is asleep.

"So, Captain, your job is to track him down. Bring him in peaceably if you can. If you can't... well, I'm sure you'll do your best.

You already have Sergeant Major Coffin with you and... Lieutenant Warwick. I s that correct?"

"It is, Colonel."

Leavenworth picked up his notes, stared at them for a moment, and then continued. "You're to take command of Company K, 120 officers and men. They're all veterans, not of the war of course; been out here on the plains for two or more years, most of them. They know the territory well. Lieutenant Glendon Daly, another Irishman, will be your second-in command, and will command the First Section. You can rely on him without reservation. Good man, Daly, good man.

"You will also be provided with three Indian scouts, a Shoshone and two Apache. Daly knows them well, been with him a while. The Shoshone language is very similar to Comanche, so you should be able to make good use of that one. His name is Bear Claw; he speaks good English. The Apaches... I have no idea what they are called, probably wouldn't be able to pronounce their names anyway," he said, with a grin.

"Sir," O'Sullivan said, thoughtfully, "would it not be a good idea to get Lieutenant Daly in here? I need to meet him anyway, an' he probably would have some ideas."

24

Leavenworth nodded, rose from his seat, and opened the office door. "Sergeant Walker. Please go and find Lieutenant Daly and have him join us as soon as possible.

"Now, Captain," he said, returning to his seat behind the desk. "Where were we? Oh, yes.

"Lieutenant Warwick will also join you and will command the Second Section. Sergeant Major Coffin will act as your first sergeant, Top Soldier. There are three other sergeants in Company K, all of them competent and reliable. I am also of a mind to attach a section of artillery; perhaps a mountain howitzer, maybe two, but I'll need to think about that some more.

"Ah, Lieutenant Daly; come in, come in. I'd like you to meet Captain O'Sullivan, the new officer commanding Company K."

Daly was a heavy-set man with graying hair and a neatly trimmed beard above which fat cheeks, dark red like over-ripe apples, gave his face a jolly, happy appearance. He was quite a bit older than O'Sullivan expected. He estimated him to close to forty years old, almost the same age as himself.

"Good to meet you, Captain. First Lieutenant Glendon Daly, at your service, sir," Daly said, standing to attention.

He was a tall man, taller even than O'Sullivan, over six feet two inches.

"At ease, Lieutenant," Leavenworth said, walking around his desk, heading for the door. "Pull up a chair;

talk among yourselves for a moment. I need to go talk to Walker for a moment."

"So, Lieutenant," O'Sullivan said, when Leavenworth had left the room, "where are you from?"

"A little place called Bantry, on the southern coast. An' yourself, sir?"

"Bantry, is it? An' me from Cork. It's a small world, so it is. When did you get here?"

"I stepped off the boat in '42 at the fine old age of fifteen years. An' you?"

"A year later, '43. I won't tell you how old I was, but I can give you a year, or two," O'Sullivan said, with a grin. How long have you been in the army?"

I joined in '61, just after Fort Sumter. I expected to fight the Rebs, but they sent me out here instead. Had a run in or two with Quantrill, an' one with Stirlin' Price, but mostly I've been out here on the plains, protectin' the Trail. Did you see any action durin' the war?"

"Hah, did I? Too much, far too much. Makes me sick just to think about it. It was a bad war, a very bad war, so it was. You are a lucky man, Lieutenant."

The two men were not alone for many minutes before they were joined once more by Colonel Leavenworth.

"I've arranged for you to inspect your new command, Captain," Leavenworth said. "They will fall in, with their mounts and equipment, at one o'clock this afternoon. You'll see to it, Lieutenant, yes?"

"I will, sir."

"Good, now back to work." Leavenworth rose again from his seat and turned to face the wall and the large map thereon. O'Sullivan remembered it well.

"Mr. Daly is, of course, more than familiar with the situation here, so most of what I am about to say will be for you, Captain; but you, Lieutenant, can feel free to offer any nuggets of wisdom that may occur to you along the way.

"You already know the main routes of the Santa Fe Trail, Captain, but what you probably don't know is the disposition of the enemy.

"There are six bands of Comanche spread all across the plains from here to here, an area of more than two thousand square miles." He swept the flat of his hand across the map from Great Bend all the way to northern Texas.

"These two blue lines, as you know, represent the Mountain Branch and Cimarron Route of the Santa Fe Trail. That, gentlemen, will be your sphere of operations."

Daly smiled, knowingly.

O'Sullivan stared at the map, glumly. "Bloody hell," he said, quietly. "Where do we start?"

"That, Captain," Leavenworth said, still staring at the map, "is the big question. White Eagle was here at Fort Dodge the middle of last month. Before that, he was up here, close to Trinidad, beyond the Raton Pass. He hit a hunting camp here, some twenty miles to the northwest of Cimarron. Now, I say he was seen at all of those places, but we don't know with absolute certainty that it *was* him. There are a half-dozen bands of Cheyenne to the north, up here, that rove all across this area." He again waved his hand across a section of the map. "That attack, any of them really, could have been made by any one of them. So... well... it's anybody's guess as to where he might be."

"Lieutenant," O'Sullivan said, turning in his chair to face Daly, "Colonel Leavenworth tells me you know this country, and the Comanche, better than anyone. Where would you start?"

"Well, White Eagle's smart," Daly said, thoughtfully. "He can always be expected to do the unexpected. The man has also hit several other small settlements and at least two stagecoach stations that I know of." He looked at Leavenworth, who was nodding his head in agreement, for confirmation. "So, if we do this.... Sir, can I have a piece of paper and something to draw with, please?"

Leavenworth handed him a large sheet of paper and a pen and inkwell. Daly dragged his chair up to the front of Leavenworth's desk and began to draw.

"If we do this...." Daly drew the two lines representing the two branches of the Santa Fe Trail.

"And then this...."

He marked several small crosses on his map, and labeled and dated them.

"And then this...."

He drew lines connecting each one of the crosses, creating a visual timeline.

"We can see that he is crisscrossing back and forth and up and down all across the territory." He looked first at Leavenworth, and then at O'Sullivan, and the lines again, as if expecting an answer. Receiving none, he continued.

"All I'm saying is that he seems to be traveling great distances between each hit. My guess is that his next attack will be somewhere in this area here." He drew a circle on his map.

"Bloody hell, man," O'Sullivan blurted. "That must be about 150 square miles, and you're only guessin', so you are. How in the name of Mother Mary are we supposed to cover an area like that with a single company of cavalry? An' one more thing: I don't see the site where Quintana killed his family, or the one where we found the dead horses."

"Well," Leavenworth said, gloomily. "I didn't say it was going to be easy." He looked at the clock on the wall. "That's about all I have time for right now. You should prepare to meet your command, Captain. And while you're about it, you might consider talking to the scouts, see if they have any ideas. I'll see you both back here at four-thirty this afternoon. Please think about your assignment, Captain, and don't be afraid to ask for help."

O'Sullivan and Daly rose from their seats, saluted the colonel, and left him alone in his office, still staring at his map.

Outside, on the front porch, O'Sullivan turned to Daly. "Has anyone tried to reach out to White Eagle, talk to him?"

"It's been tried, but he doesn't trust the army, or anyone else for that matter, an' not just because of what happed back in April. There was the Sand Creek incident toward the end of last year. A bad business that was, an' a couple more incidents besides."

"Sand Creek? What was that about?"

"Well, it wasn't the Comanche involved in that one. It was the Cheyanne and the Arapaho, but the Indian nations, even though they are constantly fighting one another, all have a common code of honor, an' they all hate the white man.

"With regard to Sand Creek," Daly continued, "the U.S. Government in Washington had assured the Cheyenne and Arapaho that they would be left alone in the territory they were occupying in southeastern Colorado. Then came the white settlers, an' the Indians didn't like it. They appealed to the government, tried to get the settlers to leave, but no, so they took matters into their own hands. Several settlements were attacked and some white folks were killed, an' a couple of children were kidnapped. The upshot of it was that the militia was sent in – well, it wasn't quite as simple as I'm makin' it sound. The militia attacked a Cheyenne and Arapaho village at Sand Creek, killed almost two hundred, most of 'em women and children. The word spread throughout the Indian nations that the U.S. Government couldn't be trusted. Now most of 'em won't talk."

"Hmmm, I see," O'Sullivan said, "at least, I think I do. Tell me, Lieutenant, what sort of man is Colonel Leavenworth?"

Daly looked sharply at him. "He's a good man, Captain, an' fair, more administrator than commander, but he knows Indians, an' he knows the plains better than most. Why do you ask?"

"No good reason, just curious. It's always a good thing to know your superiors. I must admit, though, that I'm a little surprised by his approach to this White Eagle problem. It seems to me he's thinkin' he'll leave it mostly up to me. Did you get that idea?"

"Oh yes." Daly smiled. "That's Colonel Leavenworth. He believes in delegation, so he does. An' White Eagle is not the only problem he has on his mind. There are problems with the Cheyenne an' the Arapaho to the north an' west. You'll find as you get to know him that he expects his officers to be able to handle their assignments without his having to interfere, get involved. He'll tell you what he wants, an' then he'll expect you to get it done. He'll also expect you to keep him informed, as best you can. He'll be there if you need him, but... well, you get the idea. Just don't let him down."

"Hmmm, that's unusual, so it is. Most senior officers want to manage every little detail. I'm not used to such... such... freedom. It'll take a little gettin' used to."

"Oh you'll get used to it soon enough, an' you'll like it, not havin' him breathin' down your neck, but, as I said: don't let him down."

O'Sullivan nodded, thoughtfully. "All right, Lieutenant." He consulted his pocket watch. "I'll take your word for it. In the meantime, we have a couple of hours, at least, before the parade. I'd like you to get to know the two people I brought with me, Second Lieutenant Dil Warwick and Sergeant Major Coffin."

Daly nodded. "Good idea. We can use your office."

"My office? I have an office?"

Daly smiled. "That you do, Captain, an' why not? You do need a place to hang your hat, among other things. It's over there, at the end of K Company barracks. Come, I'll show you."

Chapter 3

High on top of a bluff, deep among the peaks and valleys of the Sangre de Cristo Mountains, west of Trinidad in Colorado Territory, Chief White Eagle stood alone, preferring the solitude of the vast open space that lay before him. The leather fringes of his buckskin leggings flapped in the freshening easterly breeze, and the feathers of his headdress rustled and fluttered. The mountains stretched endlessly away into the far distance, a seemingly limitless ocean of desolation, a barren unfriendly sea of undulating ridges, scarps, cliffs, canyons, arroyos, rifts, and bluffs. He saw but he did not see; he heard but he did not hear. He was at one with the spirits of his ancestors, seeking guidance for what he knew must be done.

His arms, wrapped with colored, beaded bands of rawhide, hung loosely by his sides. He was not yet fifty years old, yet his hair was already streaked with gray. His face, thin and heavily lined, was streaked with black war paint that circled a pair of deep-set, bird-like eyes. His skin was the color and texture of buffalo hide that had been too long in the sun. His chest, also streaked with black paint, was bare, tight, and muscular, marred only by a single scar, a thin white line that ran across his belly from one side to the other.

The mid-day sun beat relentlessly down on the rocks and stone, and the horizon shimmered and wavered in the haze. He had been there since early morning; he'd watched the sun as it rose in the eastern sky. His questions had not been answered. The Great Spirit had not spoken to him, and he wondered if it might be an omen. He didn't know, nor did he care. In fact, he felt nothing other than the all-consuming need for revenge raging inside him.

He thought of his son, and of his granddaughter, all that had been left to him when Kimama, his Shoshone woman, had died from the white man's pox. They were all gone now, Small Bear and Mimiteh, killed by the white soldiers in gray. Ayasha, killed by blue coats at Sand Creek, her throat slashed, scalped, and....

He shuddered as a cold wind blew across his soul; yes, an omen. He bowed his head, then looked up, tilted his head as far back as it would go, raised his arms, and muttered a silent prayer:

Oh Great Spirit give me the strength and wisdom to protect my people from the blue coat soldiers, to defeat my enemies, to take revenge upon those who have harmed my people, and to evade and thwart those who would hunt us. All of this I beg of you, Great Spirit. But if it is not to be, then so be it. I will come to you gladly with joy in my heart.

For several moments more he stood on the cliff top, watching the fast-moving clouds, waiting for a sign from his God, but none came.

Sadly, and with a heavy heart, he turned and walked down the mountain, into the small river valley, and back to his village. Tomorrow, he would lead his warriors on yet another raid against the white man.

Chapter 4

To call the small room that had once been the company sergeant's living quarters an office was a bit of a leap. It was some sixteen feet square with a second, even smaller, room set off to the right.

O'Sullivan's new "headquarters" were somewhat sparse. What little furniture there was consisted of a large, extremely battered wooden desk and a half-dozen equally battered chairs. One sat in front of the desk, one behind it, and the others arranged "tastefully" around the walls. The floor was bare wooden planks, as were the walls and ceiling. One small window offered a somewhat restricted view of the parade ground and the gates beyond. It wasn't much, nevertheless, O'Sullivan had a feeling that, perhaps at last he had found a home, and he smiled. At last a place to call his own.

"Hah, I never had an office before."

"Mornin', Captain. Mornin, Lieutenant."

O'Sullivan turned to find a man standing in the open door to the second office. "An' good mornin' to you, too. An' who might you be?"

"That would be Corporal Haig, Captain," Daly said, before the corporal could reply. "He's your own personal Jack of all Trades, an' a bloody good one, too. An all-around useful son of a bitch, if I may say so."

Haig was indeed all that Daly professed him to be. An average sort of man of Scottish decent, he hailed from originally from Peru, Indiana. He was twenty-seven years old, and a little over five feet eleven inches tall. His face was clean-shaven. His dark brown hair was cut just long enough to touch his collar. When outdoors, he kept it in place under a standard-issue cavalry kepi. Haig was an outgoing individual, almost to a fault, with an innate ability to join in any and every conversation he might overhear, including those of his superiors. His sense of humor was legendary among those with whom he served. There were times, however, when he knew well enough to keep his mouth shut and his ears open. He also liked a drink, more than he probably should, but he was a tenacious, inventive, and conscientious soldier who could be relied upon to get the job done, whatever that job might be.

"Sir, if you'll permit me," Daly said and, without waiting for a response, continued, "Haig, go an' find Lieutenant Warwick an' Sergeant Major Coffin, an' have them join us here, as soon as possible."

"Yes, sir. Of course, sir. But–"

"Now, Corporal. We're waiting."

Haig disappeared, and Daly turned to O'Sullivan. "I'm sorry, Captain. Haig can be a bit of a trial, until you get to know him."

O'Sullivan smiled. "I understand, Lieutenant, that I do. But it might interest you to know that I spent four years as a sergeant major, an' I had to deal with hundreds just like him. In future, let me handle the men. No offense, Glen, but the men need to respect me, and I can't have you speakin' for me. Is that all right?"

Daly blushed and nodded. "My apologies, Captain. I meant no—"

"I know you didn't, an' none taken, an' don't you go gettin' any wrong ideas. I'm as easy goin' as they come, in private, that is. We're goin' to get along just fine, you an' me, that we are." He slapped Daly on the shoulder, sat down behind his desk, leaned the chair back against the wall, put his hands behind his head, and both feet on the desk.

"It a bit bloody bare," he said, looking around the office. "Must get... Haig, you said, Haig to dress it up a little."

No sooner had he said it than the erstwhile Corporal Haig stuck his head inside the door. "They are on their way, Captain." Then he turned and made as if to return to his own office.

"Not so fast, Corporal. I need some supplies, paper, pens, ink, and a map, like the one in Colonel Leavenworth's office. And I'd like you put another desk in your office for Sergeant Major Coffin. Can you handle that?" O'Sullivan asked.

"I have most of what you need in my office; the map... well, of course. I'll run over to the quartermaster an' see if he has one. If not... well, I'll get you a map, sir, never you mind about that, an' a desk, too." Haig disappeared into his office.

"The hell if he don't remind me of me old Corporal Coffin, now Sergeant Major Coffin. Now there was a character. Shame his makin' Top Soldier changed all that. Now he's all spit an' polish, so he is. But now, there's Corporal Haig, an' I'm thinkin' it's gonna be just like old times. I might just take Mr. Haig under me wing." O'Sullivan grinned at Daly, who didn't quite know what to make of his new commanding officer.

Haig returned a moment later with an armful of supplies. He dumped them in the middle of O'Sullivan's desk and was gone before either Daly or O'Sullivan could say a word.

He returned less than ten minutes later, just as Coffin and Warwick were arriving. Together, the four men watched as Haig pinned a large map on the wall behind O'Sullivan's desk. It was larger and more detailed than the Colonel's. O'Sullivan couldn't help but wonder where it had come from, but he thought it was probably better not to ask.

"Can we have some coffee, Corporal, if you please?"

The coffee duly arrived, by which time the two officers and Coffin were seated in front of the desk, the introductions having already been made.

"Bejesus, if I don't already love that man, Haig. I think I just might have found your replacement, Boone," O'Sullivan said with a grin.

Coffin smiled and shook his head, knowingly.

"Now then, Lieutenant Daly, why don't you jump up and explain to the lieutenant and sergeant major what we know. What *you* know, that is?"

Daly did as he was asked. He didn't know much more than Leavenworth, but he did raise one or two interesting points. The first was his idea of where White Eagle's village might be. The second was where he thought he might strike next. Both ideas were little more than conjecture, but it was, as he said, as good a place as any to make a start.

He sat down again, and O'Sullivan rose to his feet and turned to face the map.

"All right," he said, staring at the map. "Let's think about it like this. This is roughly where Quintana murdered White Eagle's people." He pointed to a spot on the map. "An' this is where we found the dead ponies." Again, he pointed to another spot on the map, and then he thought for a moment, the forefinger of his right hand to his lips.

"We know that White Eagle came from the southwest to recover his dead, an' so the chances are that his village is somewhere in the mountains in this area." He circled a spot on the map with his finger, roughly due west of the massacre site and south of the site where they found the dead ponies. "What do you think?"

"What you say, Captain, is probably true, but the Indians Quintana killed were on the move," Coffin answered. "We found what was left of their travois, an' if they were on the move, we have several more questions to ask. Why were they on the move? Were they moving to another location? Were they coming back from visiting yet another location? An', if they were moving their village, where were they going? An' if they were, their old village may by now have been abandoned."

"Bejesus, Boone." O'Sullivan shook his head. "You ain't makin' things any easier, an' of course you're right. There's only one thing for it – we'll have to go and take a look. It will make a good first outing for the Company." He looked at his pocket watch and noted the time, almost one o'clock. "Let's go take a look at 'em. Then I'll run it by the Colonel. Let's go."

By the time they reached the parade ground in front of the command office, Company K was already assembled and in in line.

They were quite a sight: 118 men and horses, not counting Daly and Haig, plus the three Indian scouts, all fully equipped with packs, saddlebags, and weapons. Each man stood rigidly to attention alongside his horse and carried a .52 caliber Sharps carbine, a .44 caliber Colt Army revolver, and standard-issue cavalry saber. O'Sullivan was impressed. This was his first real command, notwithstanding the short period after the Battle of Franklin, when he had taken over command of the sadly depleted 51st Indiana Volunteer Infantry Regiment. He felt an undeniable surge of pride as looked them over.

Together, he, Daly, Warwick, and Coffin stood facing them on the front porch of the command office.

Daly duly introduced the other three to the Company, and then the four of them walked down the steps to the parade ground.

The inspection was a cursory one, little more than a walk along the long line of soldiers, O'Sullivan leading. He offered a word of hello here and there, a question or two, and then he stepped back up onto the porch, turned and faced the assembly.

"Well now," O'Sullivan said, his voice just loud enough for all to hear. "We will be spendin' a whole lot of time together over the next several months, an' maybe a whole lot longer than that.

"First Lieutenant Daly," he continued, "you all know well; the rest of us you do not. I came up through the ranks, so I know your problems, feelin's, and routines. You'll find me easy enough to get along with, provided you do your job, an' do it well. Second Lieutenant Warwick is a graduate of West Point, but we won't hold that against him." The men snickered. "Now Sergeant Major Coffin, here, is quite another story. He will be Top Soldier of Company K. You will obey him at all times, officers included." He looked at Daly and then at Warwick. "He is an experienced veteran of four years of bloody warfare, six major battles, including Shiloh, Stones River, Chickamauga, Franklin and Nashville. He knows soldierin' better than any man I know, and I trust him with my life, have done for the past four years. You can, too. In fact, I wouldn't be here now if it weren't for him. Any objections? Any questions? None! Good.

"I have no idea of how much you know about our assignment, or how little," O'Sullivan continued. "I'm sure the grapevine has provided you with more information, good or bad, than you probably need to know. However, we'll be leavin' here at sunup tomorrow on our first patrol together. Rations for six days, Sergeant Major, an' fifty rounds of ammunition per man. Do not be late on parade. Dismissed!"

Sergeant Major Boone Coffin was more than a little uncomfortable listening to O'Sullivan sing his praises and realized that his life had changed forever. For all of his years as a soldier, he had kept himself to himself, kept a low profile. During his years among the lower ranks, he had turned inconspicuous into an art form. He was, or at least he had been, a master of invisibility, an enterprising, unobtrusive scrounger. He'd had no master other than the then Sargent Major O'Sullivan whom, long ago, had recognized the worth of the resourceful little soldier and taken every advantage of him. It had been a truly symbiotic relationship, but no more. Coffin's sudden elevation to the rank of Top Soldier had changed all that, and he was not sure it had changed for the better. Still, there was no going back now. Many years ago he had cast his lot with O'Sullivan and, for better or worse, he was stuck with it. *An' it had best be for the better.*

That afternoon, at four-thirty, O'Sullivan and Daly met once again with Colonel Leavenworth.

"So, gentlemen," Leavenworth said, leaning back in his chair. "What are your thoughts?"

"Well, it's like this, Colonel," O'Sullivan began. "We, that is I, have no real idea of exactly where we should begin. But we have to start somewhere, so we do, an' my thought is that the site of the massacre of White Eagle's folks would be as good a place as any. We'll head out for Fort Dodge in the morning. We'll make that our base of operations for the next several days, take another look at the massacre site, and then head up into the mountains. There's no point, I'm thinkin', in going back to where we found the dead ponies, but his village has to be somewhere up there, quite close to the massacre site, maybe ten, twenty miles. That would put it somewhere here." He rose from his seat and walked to the map.

Leavenworth swiveled his chair and looked up at the spot on the map to which O'Sullivan was pointing.

"If it's there," O'Sullivan continued, "I'll find it. If not... well, it's a start." He returned to his seat and sat down.

Leavenworth stared intently over the desk at him. "It make sense, what you say, Captain. But I fear White Eagle will be long gone when, and if, you do find his village. Still, as you say, we have to start somewhere. I'll send a dispatch to Fort Dodge, tell Captain Pearce to expect you. The fort is still under construction, but decidedly more complete that it was when last you were there."

Leavenworth stood, as did O'Sullivan and Daly. Then he walked around his desk and shook both of their hands.

"Captain," Leavenworth said, earnestly, "I'm glad to have you here. I want you to know that you have my full support. You have *carte blanch* to do whatever you think is necessary to bring White Eagle to heel, to stop these murderous attacks. I do, however, want you to keep me informed as much as possible as to your progress. I know that will not always be possible, but I expect you to communicate as best you can, and whenever you can. Good luck, Captain." He took a step back and saluted.

Daly and O'Sullivan returned the salute, spun on their heels, and left the office.

Once outside, they paused on the command office front porch, looked at one another, and grinned. With a spring in their steps, they descended to the parade ground and together they walked to O'Sullivan's office.

Chapter 5

Newsom's Station, Santa Fe Trail, July 26

Jake Newsom awoke before sunup, as he usually did. The Overland Mail stagecoach was due to leave as soon as it was light enough to see the way ahead, in order to dodge the deep ruts in the hard-packed dirt road.

Newsom's Station was just one of many small stops along the Mountain Branch of the Santa Fe Trail – a lonely dot on the map on between Fort Lyon to the north, the Raton Pass to the south. It was, as far as Newsom was concerned, a desolate, god-forsaken spot, and he often wondered why his now long deceased father had decided to put down his roots this far away from... anywhere. True, the little station made money. It was, after all, positioned right at the point on the trail where the stagecoaches reached the end of their day, although some would push on for another ten miles to the much larger Old Bent's Fort, not a military outpost, but another rest stop along the Trail.

Newsom's Station was, in fact, a very pleasant, if remote, location. Surrounded as it was on two sides and to the rear by the cliffs, bluffs, scarps, canyons, and arroyos of the Sangre de Cristo Mountains, with the wide and endless Santa Fe Trail to the front, there was a stark beauty about the place. Perhaps it was not the best choice of a place to settle down, but it was easy on the eye nevertheless.

The station was set back about fifty yards from the main Santa Fe Trail. To the sides and rear was all open ground, a flat, sandy area that stretched for more than sixty yards in each direction from the edge of the compound to end abruptly at the sheer walls of rock that rose, in places, more than a hundred feet. These were not natural walls; they were the result of several months of blasting by Jake's father when he had cleared the area in preparation to build the station. The wall was unbroken, except for an opening some seventy feet wide that gave access to a narrow arroyo, a cleft in the terrain wherein, at the center, was the dry bed of a mountain stream that flowed only during the rainy season. The arroyo meandered westward and upward through the peaks and valleys until, many miles farther on, it gave way to the high plains above the Sangre de Cristos.

The station boasted a well-stocked hardware store and grocery, a two-story wood-built residence – Jake Newsom's home – and a single story, two-room bunkhouse used primarily to bed stagecoach passengers down for the night, but also any other wanderers that might happen by. A second, smaller bunkhouse provided a home, if temporary, for the five civilian guards for whom Newsom provided room and board. Their wages were paid by a coalition of stagecoach companies. The military escorts had to make do with their tents. There was also a corral with shelter for up to twenty horses. All of this was enclosed within a rudimentary and somewhat flimsy wooden stockade. A watchtower at the northeast corner of the stockade was used by the guards to keep watch along the Trail.

Newsom was a tough and grizzled frontiersman; he'd lived all of his forty-four years on the Trail. He wasn't married, had no children, but he did employ a black woman, Elva.

Elva, one-quarter Apache, was a tall, slender woman of about thirty years of age. She wore her straight, long black hair in a thick braid that hung down her back almost to her waist. Her skin was smooth and blemish free, the milk chocolate color light for a black woman. Her eyes were the color of honey, and her breasts, though small, were clearly defined beneath her simple, brown cotton dress drawn in at the waist by a wide leather belt. Her legs, bare from the knee down, were slim and muscular. On her small feet, she wore soft, buckskin moccasins.

Of Elva's background, Newsom had no idea, and she would never talk about it. She had appeared at the station one day more than five years ago, on foot, with a small tote of personal belongings, and asked Newsom for a job. He had agreed, and she had quietly settled in. She went about her daily chores from that day to this, never saying much, never asking for anything other than her small personal needs, happy enough to have a roof over her head and small weekly wage, of which she spent very little. Neither did she have any trouble with the guards, or Newsom for that matter, although on one or two rare occasions.... There was just something about her... and, for the most part, they gave her a wide berth. Her duties were to handle the day-to-day operation of the store when Newsom was otherwise indisposed, which he often was, cook meals for the guards and guests, and to keep the station clean and tidy.

Thus it was, on that balmy Wednesday morning in late July that the Overland stage and its small military escort left the station, heading south. The coach, packed with passengers, mail, and assorted goods and luggage, set off along the Trail toward the Raton Pass and would arrive, eventually, in Santa Fe, New Mexico Territory. The time was a little before seven o'clock, the sun was up, a stiff breeze was blowing across the mountains, and all was well with the world. At least Jake Newsom thought it was as he watched the departing stagecoach disappear around the bend and over the ridge, but Newsom was not the only one watching the stagecoach leave the station that morning.

High on a ridge above and some two hundred yards to the west of Newsom's Station, White Eagle and two of his minor chiefs, Yellow Crow and Broken Nose, also watched the Overland Mail leave. He had no interest in the stagecoach. What he wanted was the horses in the station corral, the guns and ammunition in the store, and something more....

White Eagle was ready for battle. His chest was bare, and his face was streaked with black war paint. On his head, he wore the bonnet of a Comanche war chief: fifty black-tipped eagle feathers, each crowned with a red plume; the brow band was decorated with red and black beads and adorned with the down of ten eagle chicks; the down was also dyed red. Ten thin strips of buckskin, bleached, and then painted black and red, hung from two small, black and red beaded discs, one on either side of the brow band. The bonnet was uncomfortable. It was new, a replacement for the one he had lost to the gray-coat soldiers four months earlier. All three men were armed with rifles and lances.

White Eagle was in no hurry. For almost an hour after the coach had left, he and his two subordinates sat together on the bluff, watching. It was a time for thought and reflection. Neither of the two warriors dared to interrupt his thoughts. After a while, he explained his plan to them. They nodded their heads, looked at each other, and smiled.

Finally, White Eagle stood, turned to Yellow Crow and nodded. The Comanche also stood, and then raised his lance in the air in salute and ran to his pony. With a single bound, he leaped up onto its back and galloped away through the arroyo toward the west. White Eagle and his lone companion stayed where they were on the bluff, hidden by a rocky outcrop, watching the station. He waited, but not for long. Less than twenty minutes after Yellow Crow had galloped away, he reappeared, this time at the head of a band of fifteen warriors. They charged out of the arroyo and headed for the station at full speed, whooping and yelling as they went.

Jake Newsom and his five guards were all seated around a large wooden table in the kitchen of his residence when they heard the noise outside. Elva was cooking breakfast. Jake was eating fried bread, eggs and bacon. The guards were drinking coffee and waiting to be served their meal.

At first, none of them realized what they were hearing, but not for long.

"REDSKINS," Jake shouted, as he leaped to his feet and pulled the revolver from his waist.

The guards also jumped to their feet and grabbed their weapons. Elva ran out of the kitchen and hid in the root cellar.

Dumbfounded, Jake Newsom couldn't figure out what could have gone wrong. Indians were attacking the station? Such a thing had never happened before. His relationship with the local tribes had always been a good one; they all got along together well. They traded at the store, skins for the goods they needed, and they would sit around the station and smoke, and sometimes drink a little whiskey. Now this? He had to stop it.

Jake laid his revolver on the kitchen table and ran out of the front door, waving his arms in the air. Barely had he stepped onto the wooden planks of the front porch than he was hit in the shoulder by a .52 caliber Minnie ball from Yellow Crow's Sharps carbine. He went down, spinning backward from the impact, slamming his head against the door post. He struggled for a moment, tried to sit up, then lapsed into unconsciousness and fell back onto the floor, blood oozing from his wound.

Newsom was followed out of the front door by two of his guards. They were greeted by a hail of gunfire and were shot down almost before they cleared the doorway. The other three men ran to the back door, out into the compound, and made a run for the horses. Two of them didn't make it much farther than the rail fence that formed the corral. The third man, Jed Robbins, made it all the way to the fence, threw himself over it, and rolled across the sandy ground among the stamping feet of the now panicking horses. Lying flat on his back, with his arms flailing, he reached up, grabbed a halter rope, and swung himself up onto the animal's bare back. He slammed his heels into the horse's flanks and, with a wild leap, the horse was over the rail, almost losing his him as it went, through the open gates. He headed out onto the Santa Fe Trail, at full gallop, toward Fort Lyon almost eleven miles away to the north, Robbins barely managing to stay on its back.

Yellow Crow laughed aloud as his party fired wildly after him, but with no intent to do him harm. The man tore along the Trail at full speed, whipping the horse with the butt end of the halter rope as he went, urging it on, faster and faster.

High on the ridge, White Eagle sat astride his pony and watched as the white man fled toward the fort. He, too, smiled.

Moments later, he smiled again, this time as Yellow Crow dragged the black woman, squirming and squealing, from the dwelling. Yellow Crow looked up at White Eagle on the ridge, raised his right fist in the air while holding Elva by the hair with his left, and then, with a shove, he sent the woman staggering forward, down the steps to fall on her face, sobbing in the dust. White Eagle turned to look at Broken Nose, still at his side, and nodded in satisfaction, a tight, grim smile on his lips.

Jed Robbins arrived at Fort Lyon less than thirty minutes later after a wild and terrifying bareback ride. He hurtled through the open gates at full gallop, hauled on the halter rope, jerking the horse's head around to the left, and brought the heaving, sweating animal to a sideways, skidding halt outside the command office front door. So violent was the stop that he was thrown sideways off the horse's back, down onto the hard-packed dirt, where he landed on his back, driving what little air was left out of his body.

For a moment, he lay on his back, totally winded. As he struggled to sit up, the office door was thrown open and the duty officer, a captain, ran down the steps and lifted him to his feet.

"Indians, at Newsom's Station," Robbins gasped. "They done kilt Jake, an' most of the others, too. They got his woman, too, I bet. Not more'n twenny minutes ago. I come as fast as I could. Damned lucky I was to get away." He was bent forward, head down, hands on his knees, gasping for breath.

"How many of them were there?" the captain, asked, urgently.

"A dozen, no more'n a dozen; took us by surprise."

"Stay here. I'll be back."

The captain came running back yelling orders a few minutes later. Within fifteen minutes, he was mounted and at the head of a column of thirty troopers clattering out of the fort and onto the trail, heading south toward Newsom's Station. These men were hardened, veteran Indian fighters. All of them, including the captain, had been a part of the Sand Creek massacre less than eight months earlier. They would, the captain figured, have little trouble mopping up a dozen renegade Indians, if they were even still there when they arrived.

Yellow Crow's warriors rounded up and calmed the fifteen horses that were still inside the corral. They led them out of the compound and then westward into the arroyo. They took Elva, a dozen or so rifles, including four Spencer seven-shot repeaters, and several hand guns along with a half-dozen boxes of assorted ammunition. They left the bodies of the dead, and the barely conscious Jake Newsom, where they lay.

As soon as the dust had settled behind the fleeing Jed Robbins, White Eagle set about putting the second part of his plan into action.

Yellow Crow and his warriors were not the only ones he had with him. Almost his entire war party, more than one hundred warriors, was waiting, hidden and out of sight, in a small box canyon at the far end of the arroyo. Most were armed with bows and arrows, and lances. A few were armed with Sharps carbines, an odd assortment of revolvers, and even a muzzle-loading Springfield rifled musket. White Eagle brought them all forward. Their ponies, the stolen goods, and Elva, now gagged and tied hand and foot, were left behind in the canyon.

He spread his force on the heights over several hundred yards among the rock and ridges of the bluff and scarps that surrounded the station. Then he returned to his vantage point on the ridge high above, and he and his warriors settled down to wait. It was still only a little after nine o'clock in the morning.

An hour later, Broken Nose nudged him with his elbow, nodded his head to indicate the direction, and together they rose up onto one knee. More than a mile down the road to the north rose a large cloud of dust. Immediately on the alert, White Eagle cupped his hands around his mouth and uttered a loud barking noise. Then he settled down again, with Yellow Crow and Broken Nose at his side, out of sight behind a natural wall of rocks and boulders.

White Eagle cranked the well-oiled lever of his Sharps carbine and opened the breach. He took a large paper cartridge from the beaded pouch at his waist, slipped it into the open breach, and slammed it closed.

He fitted a copper percussion cap onto the nipple, firmed it into place with his thumb, then pulled the hammer back to full cock, watching as the dust cloud grew larger. His two companions did the same.

Captain Marcus Crane halted the column about a quarter-mile from Newsom's Station. He sat still for a moment, listening. Nothing. He reached for his glasses, raised them to his eyes, and searched for signs of life. Nothing. Out front of the store he could see what appeared to be several bodies. He ranged the glasses back and forth, several times, surveying the peaks and bluffs that surrounded the station. Nothing.

Crane wasn't quite sure what it was, but something in his gut told him that all was not as it appeared to be. For a long moment, he sat there, his horse stamping its feet, impatient to be moving. He shook his head. Four years in the wilderness had made him cautious, sharpened his instincts, almost to a fault, but he was still alive.

"Sergeant Donald," he said, turning in the saddle. "Take six men and go take a look. Keep your wits about you; be careful."

White Eagle watched as the seven soldiers detached themselves from the column and rode slowly forward. He pursed his lips. This was not what he wanted. If the white men searched the area surrounding the station, and he knew they would, they would discover the main force

56

of his warriors in the arroyo. For once, the chief was at a loss as to what to do next. His plan had been to fall on the blue coats and kill them all, the entire detachment. That, he now knew, would not be possible. He thought for a moment, watching the seven soldiers approach, and then made his decision.

He cupped his hands around his lips and made a low whooping sound, like that of an owl. The sound echoed among through the mountains and along the Trail.

Crane heard it and knew immediately what it was – owls do not hunt in daylight.

He twisted in the saddle and shouted the bugler to sound the recall. Immediately, the harsh sounds of the call rang out. The sergeant, now within a hundred yards of the station, heard and didn't hesitate. He yelled to his men to get out of there, hauled on the reins, and tried to turn the horse, but it was too late.

BAM! BAM! BAM!

From the top of the bluff, and the ridges around the station, more than a dozen rifles opened fire. Four of the soldiers went down, right where they were, under a hail of Minnie balls. The other three men, including the sergeant, managed to turn their horses. Before they had gone more than a dozen yards, they too were cut down, sent spinning from their now galloping mounts. Sergeant Donald, already dead, his right foot caught in the stirrup, was dragged, bumping and twisting along the deeply rutted dirt trail toward the main body of the column. As the horse galloped past, a corporal grabbed the reins and pulled it to a stop. Two more men leaped down from the saddle, released what was left of Sergeant Donald from the stirrup, and laid his broken body beside the Trail.

White Eagle was not too unhappy with the results of his plan. He had hoped to kill many more of the blue coat soldiers, but seven was good. Seven was very good, and there would be more, many more. He had the rifles from the store, fourteen of them, plus those of the guards, and ammunition for all of them. He also had Elva.

He watched as the terrified horse dragged the soldier along the trail. Then he looked around the compound below, put his Sharps to his shoulder, adjusted the back-sight slightly, and BAM! He fired a ball into the squirming body of a wounded soldier who lay on his back some three hundred yards beyond the wooden buildings. The soldier jerked, rolled over sideways, and then lay still. White Eagle nodded in satisfaction, and then rose to his feet and waved his Sharps over his head – a signal to his warriors. Then he turned and ran quickly down the rocky incline to the arroyo below where his warriors were waiting for him. He swung himself swiftly and easily up onto the bare back of his pony and, with his Sharps held high above his head, led his war party at a swift canter along the narrow arroyo and away into the mountains. Elva was seated behind Yellow Crow, her arms wrapped around his waist, trying to stay on the back of the pony.

Captain Crane ordered the column to dismount and the horses to be taken to the rear. Then he dispersed his men along both sides of the road, sending some of them forward in a wide circle through the grass to the east. The rest, including himself, he moved forward along the west side of the Trail, making good use of the cover afforded by the rocky terrain.

For almost thirty minutes, Captain Crane and his men crept slowly forward toward Newsom's Station. The small scattering of buildings with its low stockade grew ever larger as they approached it. Finally, they reached the open space that surrounded the compound and could go no further without exposing themselves to whatever dangers might be lying in wait on the heights.

Crane, at the crouch behind a large boulder, held up his hand, bringing his group to a halt. He laid his carbine down beside him, rose slowly until he was standing upright, still under cover of the boulder, and waved both arms in the air, signaling for the other group to halt also.

Again, he crouched down behind the boulder, picked up his weapon, and for several moments, he stayed still, listening intently; nothing. Then he shook his head, turned, sat down on the rocky ground, leaned his back against the boulder, and signaled for his men to do the same.

"Lieutenant," he whispered, beckoning.

The officer scrambled, bent low, around the rocks, ran quickly forward, and dropped into place beside Crane.

"I hear nothing," Crane said. "You?"

The lieutenant shook his head.

"Jesus," Crane said. "Then there's nothin' for it. I'll have to go find out." He started to rise to his feet, but the lieutenant grabbed his arm.

"I'll do it." The lieutenant jumped to his feet and ran at full speed across the open space, more than fifty yards, and dived full length into cover behind Jake Newsom's residence. Nothing. He waited, listened, stood, crept around the building, took note of the dead bodies, and circled around the store. Still nothing. Except for the dead bodies, and a semi-conscious Jake Newsom, he was alone. He walked the fifty yards to the Trail and waved his arms.

Ten minutes later, the remaining members of Crane's small force walked slowly into the compound at Newsom's Station.

Crane had realized, as soon as his lieutenant had made it unscathed into the compound, what the situation was. The Comanche were gone. He knew this from experience, from the fact that the Comanche would not get involved in a firefight they knew they couldn't win. They used stealth and ambush. They hit hard, and they ran fast. Even knowing they were probably long gone, Crane was ever the careful battlefield commander.

He had no war record, as such. He had not fought in the war with the Confederacy. His entire fighting experience had been gained in the mountains of Colorado Territory and the Great Plains. He was an Indian fighter, pure and simple, and he was part of the reason why White Eagle had tried to entrap the blue coat soldiers. He and most of the garrison of Fort Lyon had been at Sand Creek, and the Indians intended to make them pay for it.

By noon, the entire area within a two-mile radius of Newsom's Station had been reconnoitered and declared clear of hostiles. The bodies of the dead guards and soldiers had been loaded into two wagons from the station yard, and Jake Newsom was... well, he wasn't dead, at least not yet. Crane's men did what they could for him. They loaded him into one of the wagons, along with the dead guards and soldiers, and the sad little party headed back along the Santa Fe Trail to Fort Lyon. Of Elva, there was no sign.

Chapter 6

White Eagle's Village, July 26

The ride from Newsom's Station to White Eagle's camp was almost sixty miles. Clinging to Yellow Crow, trying to stay on the rump of his pony, Elva endured six hours of pure, non-stop hell.

When they arrived among the teepees of White Eagle's village at around four-thirty in the afternoon, Yellow Crow threw his left leg forward and over the pony's ears. He dropped easily to the ground, leaving Elva still on the pony's back, stiff and barely able to move. Not used to long hours in the saddle, especially bareback, her muscles had locked. Her legs and arms were seared with pain as she tried to move them, and her buttocks were raw and unbelievably painful. Much to her disgust, the tears ran freely down her cheeks.

Yellow Crow laughed. He reached up, grabbed her right arm, and pulled her roughly down, causing her to scream in pain. Her feet hit the ground, her legs collapsed beneath her, and she fell, crying uncontrollably. All around her, the women and children of the village watched in amazement as the beautiful black woman struggled to her knees, and then tried to rise to her feet. Her legs would not support her, and she again fell to the ground. She was sobbing, great heaving gulps that wracked her body, sending shudders through every pain-wracked muscle. She was on her knees, both hands forward on the ground, her head hanging between her arms, her face covered by her hair, which hung almost to the dirt, the heavy braid long since come undone.

For a long moment, she stayed where she was, her muscles locked, unable to move. Then two gentle hands took her from behind, and White Eagle lifted her to her feet.

With a great effort, she shrugged away the chief's helping hands and forced herself to stand upright. She drew back her shoulders, shook her head, throwing the long hair back over her shoulders, and then stared defiantly at the watching village. Her face was streaked with dirt and tears and yet it was still strangely beautiful.

White Eagle walked around to stand in front of her; she was almost as tall as he was, and she stared defiantly into his eyes. He smiled and nodded, impressed.

"Come," he said, as he took her gently by the right arm and pulled.

She shrugged his hand away, but did as she was asked. She followed him as he walked through the village to what she realized must be his teepee. He pulled open the flap and nodded, indicating that she was to enter. She walked a few steps inside, then turned to face him, knowing what was about to happen to her.

White Eagle followed her inside, allowing the flap to fall back into place.

It was quite light inside the teepee, much lighter than she expected.

The large structure, almost twenty feet high, with a series of poles set in a circle some fourteen feet in diameter and tied together at the top. The poles were covered with buffalo hides with a large opening high among the lodge poles to let in the light and let out the smoke from the round stone fire pit at the center of the lodge. The floor was also covered with hides, and more were piled close to the walls for sleeping.

White Eagle walked slowly around her, appraising, nodding his appreciation.

"Name?" he said, standing again in front of her.

She stood rigidly erect, staring into his eyes, defiantly, and said nothing.

"Name? Please," he said, in a quiet voice.

She hesitated for a moment, surprised by his non-aggressive demeanor, then said, quietly, "Elva. My name is Elva. You speak English?"

He nodded, his face serious. He placed his right hand on his chest. "White Eagle."

She looked at him, and nodded, and then repeated, "White Eagle."

He smiled, removed his hand from his chest, turned the palm to face her, and held it just in front of, and about a foot away from, the center of her chest, in some strange gesture, the meaning of which she had no idea. Then he shook his head slowly from side to side. "No harm... you."

She looked at him, questioningly, not quite sure what he was trying to say.

He saw the question in her eyes, and nodded, waving his hand in front of her. "No harm... we not... harm you. You safe."

"You mean you will not hurt me?"

"Yes, you safe here. Comanche not harm you."

He placed the open palm of his hand on her chest. She took an involuntary step back. He then placed the palm of his hand on his own chest, tilted his head sideways, slightly, his eyes wide open in question, and said, "You my woman now."

"Oh no, no, no... NO."

He smiled, his eyes laughing at her. Then he nodded, and, still smiling, turned and walked out of the lodge. The flap fell in place behind him.

Less than five minutes later, two Comanche women entered the lodge. Elva was now sitting on a pile of skins close to fire pit. The fire was built, but not yet lit.

One of the women carried a bowl of steaming water, the other an assortment of garments. These they laid down, the bowl on the floor, the garments on the pile of skins at her side.

That done, one of them, the taller of the two, took her hand and pulled gently, urging her to her feet. Elva rose, and the woman pulled again. Elva took a step forward. The woman nodded, smiling, and then the two of them stripped her of the now tattered cotton dress, and the underwear she wore beneath it, leaving her standing naked.

Very gently, the two women washed her from head to toe. At first she felt uncomfortable, but before they were done she found herself enjoying it. The heat of the hot cloths soothed her aching muscles.

When they were finished, and they had dried her, they handed her a dark brown cotton shirt decorated with tiny colored beads, and a light, tan-colored skirt made of soft deerskin. There was no underwear. For her feet, there was a pair of deerskin moccasins.

They watched as she dressed herself. She tucked the shirt inside the skirt and drew the hide string taught, cinching it tightly to her waist.

Finally, they combed her hair, leaving it hanging loose down her back, and then they left her.

Elva, now left alone with her thoughts, sat down again on the pile of skins by the fire pit, her hands in her lap, and began to think. She knew what was coming. She also knew there was nothing she could do about it, and, maybe it was the Apache in her, but for some strange reason, she wasn't afraid.

A little later in the afternoon, the entrance to the lodge was thrown back and White Eagle, his head now bare, his face and chest cleaned of the black war paint, stepped through the opening. He was clad only in a buckskin breach cloth, leggings and moccasins. His chest was bare, his hair in long braids, hanging down on either side of his chest.

"Stand." he said to her.

She did as asked.

He looked at her, walked around her, looked at her, appraising her. He was pleased with what he saw, and not for the first time. In fact, he had seen her, from a distance, many times at Newsom's Station when his people were trading buffalo skins.

He reached out and took her hand. "Come."

He led her out of the lodge and into the center of a large open area ringed with teepees, a gathering place for his village. Many of his people were there, waiting, including Yellow Crow, Broken Nose, several more minor chiefs, a large number of braves, women and children, and seven very old men.

Elva knew something was about to happen, but she had no idea what.

White Eagle stood beside her, raised her hand high above their heads, and began to speak, still holding her hand, now down by her side again. What he was saying, she had no idea. He spoke for several minutes. When he finished, he turned, and together they walked slowly back to the lodge. The crowd in the gathering place remained silent. Their chief had just announced that Elva was now his woman, and thus she was to be protected and, as far as Comanche women could be, respected.

Later that evening, when the sun had set and the stars were bright in the night sky, she was given a meal of roasted deer meat. Then White Eagle pointed to one of the several piles of skins, indicating the place for her to sleep. That done, he laid himself down on a second pile of skins, covered himself, closed his eyes, and was soon asleep.

Elva lay in the darkness, watching the flickering shadows on the wall of the lodge, cast by the flames of fire. For a long time she lay, wondering why the chief, now her husband, so she supposed, had not taken advantage of her. Of that, she was both relieved and, more than a little horrified to realize, a little disappointed.

Chapter 7

The sun was already rising in the eastern sky when Captain Ignatius O'Sullivan stepped quickly across the packed dirt of the parade ground to where Company K and two covered wagons were already assembled and waiting. The wagons at the rear of the column were transport for the Company's rations, personal items, and spare ammunition, etc.

He was feeling more than a little self-conscious knowing that not only were there more than 120 pairs of his own men's eyes on him, but also those of Colonel Leavenworth and more than a dozen other officers who had assembled on the front porch of the command office to watch him go.

Corporal Haig, holding O'Sullivan's horse as well as his own, waited along with Coffin, Daly, and Warwick, in front of the command office.

"Have the men mount up, Sergeant Major," O'Sullivan said, briskly, taking the reins from Haig and swinging himself quickly and easily into the saddle.

"MOUNT UP! COLUMN OF TWOS!" Coffin shouted.

Leather rustled and equipment clanged as Company K took to the saddle. O'Sullivan was inordinately pleased, and not a little proud, as he watched his command swing effortlessly, almost as one, up onto their horses and maneuver them into column. He twitched the reins, swung his horse around to face Colonel Leavenworth, saluted, then turned again and trotted to the front of the column, followed by Coffin, Daly, and Warwick.

'Unfurl the colors," Coffin ordered.

The Union flag, the regimental banner, and the guidon of Company K were soon snapping in the light morning breeze, just to the rear of the officers at the head of the column.

"FORWAAARD... HO," O'Sullivan ordered, then touched his spurs to his horse's flank, urging it to a light canter. Company K rode through the gates and out into the grasslands beyond. O'Sullivan looked back at the gates of Fort Larned and heaved a silent sight of relief; he was no longer on display. The ordeal was over.

The ride to Fort Dodge took two days. It had been an easy, uneventful journey during which they had camped overnight along the way among the grasslands that bordered the Santa Fe Trail. The days were hot, the nights cool, and the camaraderie among the men was, for O'Sullivan at least, a joy to behold. After only a day in their company, he felt, for the first time in his often-turbulent military career, that he had at last found his calling. This was where he was meant to be, and it felt good.

That first night, he had sat alone in the darkness, watching the men as they went about bedding down for the night. They'd built fires, raised tents, cooked, and finally sat around singing the old songs of home and talking of loved ones left behind. His heart was full.

Finally, when all was quiet, and he had lay alone under the stars, his thoughts had turned to times past, unpleasant times of battles won and lost, images he would not soon forget. At last, he had fallen into an uneasy sleep filled with the dead and the dying, and then he awoke, cold but sweating. He looked at his pocket watch. Two o'clock in the morning. He sat bolt upright, looked around, and listened. All was quiet, except for the incessant chirping of the insects of the night. He wrapped his blanket around him, lay down with his head on his saddle, and soon drifted off into a deep, dreamless sleep.

Some hours later, he awoke with a start to the raucous sounds of the bugler playing *Reveille*. The air was soon filled with the aroma of coffee and frying bacon. Company K was already preparing for the day ahead.

They arrived at Fort Dodge at just after six-thirty in the early evening of July 27. Captain Henry Pearce was at the gate to meet them.

Fort Dodge, if it could be called a fort, was little more than a collection of sod-built structures and a rail fence around the perimeter. It was muddy, depressingly dismal, and seething with men: soldiers, engineers, workmen, and even Indians from a variety of tribes,

Shoshone, Apache, Kiowa, and more. Fort Dodge was a still a work very much in progress.

The command office was located in large, single-story adobe structure wherein Captain Pearce maintained the daily work schedule, scheduled regular patrols on the Trail and in the general vicinity of the fort, and organized escorts for the coming and goings of the various stagecoach lines. His was not the most pleasant of assignments, but he went about his work with a cheerful, upbeat disposition, and everything ran smoothly, as far as was possible under such conditions.

For more than an hour that evening, he and O'Sullivan sat and talked. They had met before, a couple of months earlier, when O'Sullivan had passed through the fledgling outpost in pursuit of a band of Confederate raiders.

Pearce was an experienced Indian fighter, having spent the previous three years at Fort Larned, and O'Sullivan took full advantage of his local knowledge.

"They tell me that you had run in with this White Eagle only last month," O'Sullivan said. "I'd like to hear about it, if you don't mind, Captain."

"Well, it wasn't much of a run in. It was all a bit one-sided, his side. They attacked after dark, late, when most of the men were asleep. It was a small war party, perhaps a couple of dozen, maybe a few more. They were after the horses, and they got 'em, too – took thirty cavalry mounts. They crept in under cover of darkness. No one heard a thing until they left with the horses, whoopin' and hollarin'. They took down a section of the rail fence at the rear. Unfortunately we had guards posted everywhere but there. They were in, out, and gone before we knew it. I sent a company of cavalry after them, but... well... in the dark, they couldn't even pick up the trail. White Eagle – and I can't say with any real certainty that it was him – got clean away. I can't imagine who else it might have been; it was typical of how he operates. He uses stealth, is a master of the surprise attack, and he will not stand and fight, unless he's sure he can win."

"Do you have any idea where his village might be?" O'Sullivan asked, staring at the map on the wall behind Pearce.

"Not for sure, but I'd bet that it's somewhere in the mountains west of the Mountain Branch of the Santa Fe Trail; has to be." He stood, turned and faced the map, drawing a circle on it with his forefinger. "Somewhere in this area, I would think, but... who knows?" He shrugged his shoulders, turned and sat down again.

O'Sullivan sighed.

"You look a little out of sorts, Captain," Pearce said, with a smile. "It's a big job."

"That it is, Captain, an' I'm a little like a bloody fish out of water, so I am. I ain't used to havin' to figure things out for m'self, always had that done for me in the past."

"Ah, the responsibility of an independent command," Pearce said, with a grin. "I understand. It's a lonely life."

"True, an' I don't mind tellin' you I have no real idea where to begin. I'm confused and befuddled. It's a huge area you pointed out on the map. Must be all of three hundred square miles of nothin' but mountains. How the hell am I supposed to find him among all that?"

"Well, it's not going to be easy, that's for sure," Pearce said. "My advice is to do as you planned. Go take a look at the two sites we know about for sure, see if those scouts of yours can pick up any signs. Look." He rose again and turned to face the map. "Here is where Quintana massacred the Comanche. This is where he slaughtered White Eagle's ponies." He pointed to each spot on the map and continued. "This here is Trinidad on the Mountain Branch, and these are Old Bent's Fort, Newsom's Station, Fort Lyon, Milton's Place, Cimarron, and there are more. There are buffalo hunters spread all over this area here. All we know for sure is where he was three months ago, when Quintana killed his ponies, right?" O'Sullivan nodded. "He'll stay away from the Trail," Pearce continued. "He has to be, in my opinion, somewhere here on the Arkansas River. Well, that's where I would start. Here, where Quintana attacked his camp."

O'Sullivan nodded, thoughtfully, then sighed. "Yep, that was my plan, too. So that's what I'll do."

Chapter 8

The Grasslands, July 31

Company K left Fort Dodge the following morning at first light. They left the wagons behind, taking with them rations for ten days loaded onto six pack mules, supplied by Captain Pearce. The wagons, O'Sullivan knew, would be unable to negotiate the steep and narrow mountain trails. It was his intent to scout the area up to and beyond White Eagle's ill-fated camp, and then return to Fort Dodge.

For six miles, they followed the Santa Fe Trail southwest, then turned off toward the mountains to the west, retracing Quintana's route of almost three months ago.

They arrived at the old campsite of May 1st four days later, just after noon on July 31. The remains of the campfire could still be seen, and the rocky draw that led to the trail up the mountain was easily identified, but that was not an option. O'Sullivan knew from his earlier experience that it was too steep for the horses, and too narrow. They would have to find another way up.

There were still at least six hours of daylight left, so O'Sullivan sent one of the Apache scouts southwest to see if he could find a better route up the mountain, and the other Apache he sent to the north. In the meantime, he decided to take the Shoshone scout, Bear Claw, and a small party, including Coffin, Warwick and Daly, through the draw and up the trail to visit White Eagle's campsite.

He gave orders for the rest of the company to make camp for the night and then he and his small party headed across the grasslands to the entrance of the draw.

The trail up the mountain was accessible on horseback for all but that final five hundred yards. With the top of the mountain in view, they tethered the horses and scrambled up the rest of the way and onto the crest of the ridge. The view from the top was stunning. As far as they could see to the east, the grasslands stretched away toward the horizon. The tiny figures of Company K could easily been seen pitching tents and going about the business of setting camp for the night.

O'Sullivan remembered vividly the trail that led to White Eagle's campsite and so, as it was still daylight, it took them no more than thirty minutes to reach it.

They approached cautiously through the trees, and O'Sullivan, as he remembered the obnoxious stench of his previous visit, could not help sniffing the air. He smiled when he saw that Warwick was doing likewise. The noxious smell was, however, gone, and so were all signs that there had ever been a campsite on the spot. The exception was the widespread carpet of bones, the remains of more than forty of White Eagle's ponies, now picked clean by the scavengers of the high plains and bleached white by the sun.

O'Sullivan asked Bear Claw to look for any signs that might indicate which direction the Comanche chief had taken. He was gone for more than an hour, and while they awaited his return, the soldiers wandered about the one-time campsite, searching. Like Bear Claw, they found nothing. Too much time had passed and the wind and weather and the profusion of wild animals had obliterated every sign there might once have been. It was disappointing, but not unexpected. And so they waited, and while they did so, O'Sullivan pulled a small, folded map from the inside of his tunic and gestured for Coffin and the two officers to sit down on a low bank on the edge of the campsite.

As they sat, Warwick stretched out his legs in front of him and placed his hands, palms down, on the grass. Feeling something strange, smooth and rounded, under his right hand, he looked down to see what it was. Two orbital eye sockets looked up at him. Startled, he snatched his hand away and jumped to his feet. There on the ground, next to where he had been sitting, was a human skull and several small bones, all but hidden by a layer of dirt and grass. They were, though Warwick didn't know it, all that remained of Confederate Private Bob Flint, Jesse Quintana's lead scout. He'd been struck down by White Eagle's lance and finished by a shot to the head from Quintana's Colt Navy revolver.

Warwick shuddered, walked a few paced to the other side of the group and sat down again, taking careful note of the ground before he did so.

"All right, then," O'Sullivan said, unfolding the map. "There's nothing left here, which is about what I expected, an' I doubt that Bear Claw will find anythin' either; it's been a long time, too long."

He spread the map out across his thighs, smoothed it, turned it a little, shook his head, nodded, and turned and looked at each one of them in turn. "Any ideas, anyone?"

"Can I?" Coffin asked, reaching over Daly and taking the map.

O'Sullivan nodded.

Coffin looked at it for a moment. "As I see it, we have little option but to go this way." He drew a line with his finger on the map. "He must have gone either north or west. There's nothin' here but this high ridge we are on now." He pointed again. "He's not going to be here; it's too accessible. My bet is that he's west of the Mountain Branch of the Santa Fe, and north of the Arkansas River, here. That's wild country up there, unexplored, mostly. If so, there's no point in trying to find a way up the mountain. It would be easier an' quicker to go back to Fort Dodge an' take the Trail, past Cimarron, an' up into the badlands to the northwest of Fort Lyon."

O'Sullivan sat quietly for a moment, thinking, then said, "Anyone else?"

"Makes sense to me," Warwick said. "We could track back and forth among these mountains for weeks and find nothing. I think Sergeant Major is right: better to start somewhere else rather than where we know he ain't. I say we go back to Fort Dodge. There may be news."

"Lieutenant Daly?" O'Sullivan asked.

"I agree. We could spend months up here an' find nothin'. To my knowledge, there hasn't been any activity in this area... well, I just ain't heard of any."

"That's it, then," O'Sullivan said, rising to his feet. "We'll wait for Bear Claw, then head back to Fort Dodge at sunup." He heaved a heavy sigh and shook his head.

"Sir, don't let this get you down," Daly said. "This is how it works: month after month of nothin', searchin', and then, maybe, we get lucky. They hit a farm, a hunting camp, even a cavalry patrol, and then we have something solid to work with. There's nothing for us out here."

O'Sullivan, somewhat mollified, nodded his agreement. "Right you are, then. Here's Bear Claw. Anythin'?" he shouted, as the Shoshone trotted quickly toward them.

Bear Claw shook his head.

"Thought so. Let's go."

Chapter 9

Buffalo Camp 70 Miles SW of Fort Dodge, August 2

Paul LeBeau and Claude Colban were at peace with the world, and with themselves. For almost a month, the two Frenchmen had been out on the Great Plains, far from civilization, what little there was of it. They'd camped between the two routes that made up the Santa Fe Trail: the Mountain Branch to the west, and the Cimarron Route to the east. The hunting had been good. More than a hundred buffalo skins lay in several piles around the campsite, some stretched on rough wooden frames, drying in the heat of the sun. The stench of rotting flesh, though the two men seemed impervious to it, was sickening.

LeBaeu and Colban were true frontiersmen: wild and rough individuals, dirty, unkempt, and stinking, their clothes stiff with dried blood and other foul fluids. They lived and worked hard, rarely played, drank hard, and they expected to die young. Now, after weeks in the wilderness, they were tired. The days had been long and the work nonstop. Mornings were spent in the grassland, hunting, killing, and skinning. The afternoons were spent scraping and framing the skins. The evenings were spent in a drunken stupor brought on by consuming copious amounts of cheap, rotgut whiskey.

Night was drawing in. The sun had already set, leaving the sky an ocean of dull red set with scudding black clouds, the harbingers of bad weather to come, but the two hunters were already in a land where little mattered other than the next sip. They had eaten dinner, gnawed on haunches of barely cooked buffalo meat, the juices thereof had only added to the rest of the mess that their clothing had become.

As the sky continued to darken, and the fire burned low, they wrapped themselves in their stinking blankets and settled down to sleep. Tomorrow, they would gather their skins, load them onto the two small carts, and head for Beckler's station to trade.

They had not been long asleep when LeBeau awoke with a start. What had disturbed him, he no idea, but whatever it was, he was experienced enough in the way of the wilderness to know that it wasn't to be ignored.

He rose quietly, shaking his head to clear it from the fug of the strong drink, reached for his Spencer carbine, and then shook Colban's arm.

Colban stirred, rolled over, and saw LeBeau crouched over him with his fingers to his lips, urging him to be silent. He nodded, rose to a sitting position, and grabbed his own Spencer. He checked the load, looked up at LeBeau, and rose to a kneeling position.

Together, the two men listened, looking around. The fire was now little more than pile of red hot embers. LeBeau threw several logs onto them and, with a shower of sparks that whirled upward into the black sky, it crackled and burst into flame.

It was a mistake. The flames cast a flickering light over the campsite, outlining the two men against the darkness. Colban did not hear the arrow that slammed into his shoulder, spinning him sideways and backward onto the hard ground beside the campfire, nor did LeBeau hear the one that a second later hit him squarely in the chest.

Colban's wound was not fatal; neither was LeBeau's, at least not immediately.

The two men lay on their backs staring up into the blackness until, only moments later, the shadows loomed over them.

White Eagle, Yellow Crow, Broken Nose, and ten Comanche warriors halted their ponies close to the buffalo hunters' campfire. The three chiefs dismounted and walked slowly to where the two men were lying, barely conscious. They stood over them, looking down, full of hatred and contempt.

White Eagle turned to the rest of his warriors, snapped his finger, and waved his hand in the direction of the piles of buffalo skins. They dismounted. Three of them held the ponies, three more began piling the buffalo skins onto the hunter's carts. The four who remained joined the three chiefs and the two hunters.

White Eagle leaned over the two men and jerked the arrows roughly out of the wounds and threw them to the ground. LeBeau barely stirred, but Colban shrieked in pain. The chief smiled; there was no humor in it. He turned and nodded. The four warriors grabbed the two men and hauled them upright in front of White Eagle. Lebeau's head hung, his chin on his chest. Colban stared, wild eyed, into the face of death: White Eagle.

The two men were stripped of their stinking clothes and tied, naked, to two of the wooden frames they had used to stretch the buffalo skins. They, too, were stretched like the skins they had collected. Their wrists and ankles were tied wide apart in the form of an X. One hung barely breathing. The other stood on legs stretched wide apart, terrified.

White Eagle stood first in front of Calban, then took a step sideways to stand in front of LeBeau. He shook his head. His eyes were no more than slits, his mouth curled in contempt at the sight of the barely alive Frenchman. He took his knife from its sheath, stepped in close, grabbed LeBeau's hair with his free hand, and jerked his head upward. With a single, backhanded flick of his wrist, he slashed the man's throat from one side to the other.

Colban groaned aloud at the sight of LeBeau's blood pumping from his neck, and he looked at White Eagle, pleading.

"You kill the *bozheena,* the buffalo, take only the skins. You come only to destroy. Now I destroy you."

Again, White Eagle stepped forward. He grabbed Colban by the hair, and jerked his head upward. With a slash of the knife, he sliced away the top of his scalp, leaving the skull exposed and blood running in rivulets down his face.

Colban screamed, but his ordeal was only beginning. All of White Eagle's pent up hatred for the white man came bursting from him as he sliced at Colban's flesh. The ritual took almost an hour, and when it was done, Colban hung, almost lifeless, bleeding profusely, on the frame.

White Eagle and his warriors melted away into the night, taking with them the two carts loaded with buffalo skins and the two Spencer rifles. Colban lasted just two hours more, hanging from the frame in the darkness, until the last flicker of light died in his eyes, and he along with it.

Two days later, a cavalry patrol out from Fort Dodge happened upon the buffalo camp. Hardened as the troopers were, they were unprepared for what they found.

The wildlife had not been kind to LeBeau and Colban. What the vultures had not taken, the scavengers of the grasslands had. The bodies hung like two grotesque gargoyles, still tied to the wooden frames. The eye sockets were now empty, bar for the maggots that infested the two corpses. Most of the flesh had been stripped away; only a few shreds of skin, tissue and muscle dried by the hot sun still clung on the bones. The stink of rotting meat permeated the air for several hundred feet in every direction.

Five of the twenty-four troopers were unable to control their heaving stomachs. Most of the rest could only stare in horror at the spectacle before them.

With bandanas wrapped around mouths and noses, they set about recovering the bodies. There were no horses left in the camp, nor skins, nor mules, nor carts. What little that remained of Colban and LeBeau was wrapped in cavalry blankets and slung across two cavalry horses whose unlucky owners rode up behind two of their fellow troopers.

The patrol arrived back at Fort Dodge two days later. It had been a very unpleasant ride.

Chapter 10

Fort Dodge, August 5

O'Sullivan and Company K arrived back at Fort Dodge just after noon after a long but uneventful ride over five days. He was angry with himself, though as far as his fellow officers and Sergeant Major Coffin were concerned, for no good reason. Still, O'Sullivan was not the most patient of men, and after what amounted to, as far as he was concerned, "ten days wasted chasing bloody rainbows," he needed something to work with, some solid information. Little did he know it was already waiting for him – not just one link to White Eagle, but two.

By late afternoon that same day, he and his officers, along with Coffin, cleaned up and dressed in fresh uniforms. After a good meal, they were seated together in Captain Pearce's offices, listening as he related the events of the past several days.

"They hit here, at Newsom's Station first, on the twenty-sixth," he began, pointing out the spot on the wall map. "Then they hit a buffalo camp, here, on the second, we think, from the state of the bodies. That's six full days after the first raid. We know they were Comanche because we recovered two arrows. Now these two locations are about eighty miles apart - two days ride, three at the most, for a war party. That leaves three, maybe four days unaccounted for, which indicates that they probably returned to their village between raids. They would not have taken captives with them on the second raid.

"Now, we know that the village is not east of the Mountain Branch, but let's suppose that their village is within a day's ride, a day and a half at the most, of Newsom's Station. That would put the village somewhere here, forty, maybe fifty miles or so west of the Santa Fe in these mountains somewhere here." He drew a circle with his finger on the map. "I'd say that would be a good place to begin... yes?" Pearce looked at the group expectantly.

"That makes sense," Daly said, thoughtfully, "but how did he get from his village, if that's where it is, to the buffalo camp? There's nothing but mountains between them."

"There's no way to know, short of tryin' to track 'em, Pearce said. "These people know the mountains and plains better than any. They grew up among 'em."

"Three days ago?" O'Sullivan asked. "That's when they hit the buffalo hunters?"

"Yes, give or take a day." Pearce nodded.

"An' how far it that from here?"

Pearce glanced at the map. "Seventy-five, eighty miles."

"So, if we left tomorrow morning," O'Sullivan asked, "we'd be there, at the camp, by when, noon on the eighth?

"Sounds about right."

"Hmmm, that'll be six days then," O'Sullivan said, thoughtfully. "Whew, six bloody days – they could have traveled at least 150 miles, probably more. Well, it won't be the first time I've had a gap like that to close, but...."

Pearce nodded. "What's your plan, Captain?"

"It's pretty damn simple. I don't see any alternative but to pick one or the other of the two attack sites an' have at it. The buffalo camp makes the most sense, it bein' the closest, an' only three days since White Eagle hit it. But by the time we get there... well, I'm wonderin' if there'll be anythin' left for us to find."

O'Sullivan was silent for a moment, "An' if we decided to try Newsom's Station? How about that?"

"That's what I would do if I were you," Pearce said, without hesitation. "And I'd take the Trail. It's a fairly easy run all the way from here to there. You can take the wagons with you, stop at Fort Lyon and resupply. The station is only ten miles from there."

"How far is that from here?" O'Sullivan asked.

"Fort Lyon is maybe 150 miles. Newsom's Station is ten miles more, so, six days, more or less."

"Holy Mother Mary. I need to think about that. He hit Newsom's Station on the twenty-sixth, you say?"

Pearce nodded in agreement.

"Then, if we go that route, we're talking ten days ago, plus six or seven more to get there. That's a total of almost seventeen days, more'n two weeks. Geeze."

"It is what it is, Captain," Pearce said, grimly. "We can only do our best. You have to pick one or the other and do what you can."

O'Sullivan nodded. "Right you are. I'll let you know later today, but, one way or the other, we will be away from here at sunup tomorrow."

A little later that same day, O'Sullivan, Coffin, Daly and Warwick were sitting together eating their evening meal. At first, the conversation was of old times and, of course, the war and the loss of President Lincoln. Soon, however, the talk turned inevitably to the task in hand.

"So," Coffin said. "Any thoughts about tomorrow?"

"That I have," O'Sullivan replied, through a mouthful of stewed cabbage. "Nothin' but thoughts, all revolvin' around in me head an' little to say for m'self." He looked at Daly. "Is the company ready for an early start, Lieutenant?"

"It is, Captain. The wagons are loaded, and five days' rations have been issued to the men."

"Wagons, so you say. Then that means you think I should go the Mountain route."

"No, Captain, just being prepared. If you decide to go that route, they are ready. If not, it makes little difference; they can be left here and unloaded after we are gone."

"Good, good thinkin'. So, let me have it, then, all of you. What are your thoughts? Which way, do you think we should go?"

At first no one spoke, then, tentatively, Warwick said, "I'm thinking the mountain route, Captain."

"Well? Go on. Why the mountains?"

"Well, Captain, it just seems to make sense. The Comanche village has to up beyond the Mountain Branch; just has to be. Newsom's Station is much closer to the buffalo camp. It... well, it just makes sense."

"Anyone else?" O'Sullivan asked, looking at Daly and Coffin.

"I agree with the lieutenant," Coffin said. "It does make sense."

"Me too," Daly said, nodding.

O'Sullivan looked grimly at each one in turn, the grinned broadly. "Just what I was thinkin'. If we go to the buffalo camp, we'll just be that much farther behind them, an' more. An' so it will be, then. Newsom's Station it is. We should be at Fort Lyon by noon, or a little later, on Thursday the tenth."

He thought for a moment, seemed about to say something else, then laid down his fork, and pushed the empty plate away toward the center of the table. He settled back in his chair, steepled his fingers and put them to his lips.

"You know, Glen," he said to Daly. "I know little enough about Indians. What is it that White Eagle wants?"

"Hah, that's easy enough to answer," Daly said. "He wants us to stop stealing their lands and killing the buffalo, and that's not going to happen. The United States Government wants rid of the Indians entirely, wants 'em put on the reservations where they say they belong. The problem is, the Indians don't see it that way, at least not anymore, not since that mess at Sand Creek. We've constantly lied to them and broken one treaty after another. Sherman has given orders that all of the tribes be rounded up and forced onto reservations that are barely big enough to hold them.

"Most of the present situation stems from the Treaty of Fort Laramie in 1851. That treaty was between the United States and a number of the tribes, mainly the Cheyenne and Arapaho, along with several smaller factions and tribes."

Daly was silent for a moment, remembering times long past, and with no little regret. "Look, Captain, there's something I have to tell you." Again, he hesitated.

"Well, out with it, man," O'Sullivan said.

"Well, sir. It's not something of which I can say I'm proud. The fact is.... I was at Sand Creek. I took part in that bloody mess. Not the killing - I didn't get there 'till it was all over - but I was a part of that campaign."

O'Sullivan looked hard at Daly, as did Coffin and Warwick. They had all heard about Sand Creek, in various levels of detail, but never a firsthand account from a witness or... participant.

"Go on, Captain," O'Sullivan said, quietly.

Daly heaved a sigh. "I suppose I'd better give you a little of the background first.

"Under the terms of Fort Laramie, the Cheyenne and Arapaho were given all the land between the North Platte and Arkansas Rivers, and from the Rocky Mountains, including the Sangre de Cristos, eastward into western Kansas, almost to Fort Zarah.

"Unfortunately, eight or nine years later, I don't know exactly when, gold was discovered in the mountains and that brought about flood of white prospectors and settlers into the Cheyenne and Arapaho territory. The Indians didn't like that and made concerted efforts to drive the white man from their lands. Anyway, to cut this short, in 1860 the United States Commissioner for Indian Affairs was sent to renegotiate the treaty.

"The new treaty reduced the Indian lands to a small part of eastern Colorado Territory, along the Arkansas River between the northern boundary of New Mexico and Sand Creek, thus separating them from the Great Plains and the buffalo. Some bands of Cheyenne and Arapaho, along with several bands of Comanche," he paused, "including White Eagle's breakaway band of Kwahadi Comanche, were opposed to the new treaty an' wouldn't sign, which is another good reason to assume that his village is somewhere up there in the mountains of southeastern Colorado Territory.

"Anyway, as I said, they were opposed to the new treaty, and they vowed to continue to live and hunt the buffalo in their old lands, in the eastern Colorado and western Kansas Territories. The white settlers and gold prospectors, however, demanded that the treaty be enforced, an' that any and all Indians who refused to abide by it would be regarded as hostile."

Again, Daly paused for a moment, taking a drink of water.

"An' that was what led to the massacre at Sand Creek in November last year."

He shook his head, seemingly lost in thought.

"Anyway," he continued, They sent in the Colorado State Militia, of which I was then a part. Colonel John Chivington was in command. This followed several Indian attacks on white settlements in the area.

"They attacked the Cheyenne and Arapaho encampment on Sand Creek." Daly shook his head. "We were under orders not to take prisoners, and we didn't; they didn't. In fact, Chivington specifically ordered that all of the Indians be killed, including the women and children, and... well, he's supposed to have said, 'Kill and scalp 'em all, big and little; nits make lice,' or something like that.

"They killed and mutilated more than 180 of them, mostly women and children. Fortunately, for me at least,

I arrived with my company just as it ended, just as the scalping was being done. Sickening. The survivors, what few there were, ran off into the mountains. We didn't pursue them, but there were several officers who wanted to hunt them all down and kill them. It didn't happen, partly, I think, because Chivington suddenly realized what he had done.

"Captain, I didn't see any of the horrors that you experienced during the war. No Shiloh, Antietam, or Gettysburg, but what I saw that day I'll never forget. The dead bodies lying around everywhere. The women, some with babies in their arms. The children – some shot, some with their throats cut.... Oh my God."

He sat quietly for a moment, his head hung, eyes closed, hands clasped together between his knees, and then he continued.

"All of that happened just nine months ago. Since then, the Cheyenne, Arapaho, and many sympathizers among the neighboring tribes, including the Sioux and Comanche, have been on the warpath. There have been several attacks on the stage stations along the Santa Fe Trail, including one at Julesburg and the one we just heard about at Newsom's Station. They've hit buffalo camps and isolated settlements, and even here at Fort Dodge, as you know. It's a mess."

"Yes, Sergeant Wilson. What is it? O'Sullivan asked he saw Pearce's duty sergeant approaching.

"Captain Pearce would like a word, sir... now, if you please."

"Does he now? Well. I'd better go see what he wants, then. You three stay here," O'Sullivan said to his companions. "I'll be back in a jiffy."

"You'll have to put off your expedition for a few days," Pearce said. "I've just received a dispatch form General Sherman. He is at Fort Larned and wants to see you."

"He wants to see *me?* An' why in God's name would he want to do that?" O'Sullivan asked.

"I have no idea. But when the man calls, it's best to come running."

"I met him once, you know," O'Sullivan said. "Didn't like him, not one little bit. The man's a bloody barbarian, so he is."

"Well, the man is now in charge of this entire department, you included, Captain," Pearce said, with a sour grin. "I can't say I envy you your visit. I hear he is tough man to talk to. No social skills and... well, he doesn't like to listen. There's only one opinion – his."

"When am I expected?"

"Now, as of yesterday," Pearce said, with a smile. "Fort Larned is sixty miles from here - a day and a half ride. If you leave at first light, you should be there by noon on Monday."

95

Chapter 11

After riding through much of Sunday night, O'Sullivan and his small escort arrived at Fort Larned at eleven o'clock on Monday morning. He spent just a few moments in his office to get himself cleaned up after the long ride, then reported to Colonel Leavenworth's command office.

"Come in," a voice called in answer to his knock on the office door.

The colonel was not there. His desk was occupied by someone O'Sullivan immediately recognized as Major General William Tecumseh Sherman.

"At ease, Captain," Sherman said, dryly, eying the rigid O'Sullivan over the huge cigar that stuck out from between his teeth. "Take a seat." He waved a hand, indicating the chair in front of the desk.

O'Sullivan sat down, his back rigid.

"I said, at ease, Captain."

O'Sullivan visibly relaxed.

"Much better. No need to stand on ceremony here. How are you, Captain? It's been a long time since last we met. Shiloh, wasn't it? You were just a sergeant back then. How are you finding the rigors of command?"

"Shiloh it was, General. As to command... it took a bit of gettin' used to, so it did."

96

Sherman nodded. "I had a long talk with General Thomas. He thinks very highly of you."

O'Sullivan merely tilted his head, slightly.

"Tell me, Captain, what do think about the Indians, about the situation out here?"

"Well, they're a problem, no doubt about that, but it seems to me that they might have something of a grievance, especially after Sand Creek and what happened to White Eagle and the hands of Quintana, but they do need to be contained."

"Ah yes, White Eagle, the reason I brought you here. Before we go any farther, Captain, you need to know that while I don't necessarily condone what happened at Sand Creek, I do consider it to have been a necessary action that they brought down upon themselves. The Indians, all of 'em – the Cheyenne, Arapaho, Kiowa, Comanche – are all murderin' savages and they got exactly what they deserved. That, Captain, is my considered opinion, and we'll not mention Sand Creek again. Is that clear?"

O'Sullivan was stunned. "So you're sayin' that the murder of innocent women and children is acceptable?"

"No, Captain. I'm not saying any such thing. What I am saying is that if it hadn't been for the actions of their leaders, Sand Creek never would have happened. They have no one to blame for what happened but themselves. These people are primitive savages, animals. Their puerile efforts to become civilized are laughable."

"But–"

"No buts, Captain. It's over, finished with. No point in rehashing what was done or how it might have been done better. Washington has decreed that the Indian problem must be solved, even if it means the total eradication of every last one of 'em. I intend to make sure that the problem is, indeed, solved."

Sherman slid open the desk drawer, reached inside, withdrew a small package, and tossed it to O'Sullivan. "Here, put those on."

O'Sullivan, puzzled, opened the package. It contained two sets of yellow and gold shoulder flashes adorned with the silver oak leaves of a lieutenant colonel of cavalry. He looked up at Sherman, eyes wide, questioning.

"It's a brevet rank," Sherman said, waving his cigar in the air, "good only until the present war with the Indians is concluded. You will have all of the authority, and responsibility of the rank, but will retain your pay as a captain. I am giving you another company of cavalry, and a section of artillery – two mountain howitzers – which will, together with your own company, increase your strength to slightly more than three hundred men, including officers and NCOs. That being so you will need the extra rank. SERGEANT WILSON."

"Yes, General?" Wilson said, sticking his head through the doorway.

"Go find Captains Carson and Morgan and ask them to report to me, immediately." He turned to

O'Sullivan. "Captain, go put those flashes on your shoulders and return here immediately."

O'Sullivan stood, saluted, spun on his heel, and left the office, stunned, bewildered, and not a little confused.

He returned to Sherman's office less than ten minutes later and found the door to the inner office closed.

"Congratulations, Colonel," Sergeant Wilson whispered with a grin, as he knocked on the office door.

O'Sullivan simply shook his head, not knowing quite how to respond.

"Tell Colonel O'Sullivan to come on in," Sherman said, in response to Wilson's knock.

Seated in front of Sherman's desk were two officers, both captains: one cavalry, one artillery.

"Colonel O'Sullivan. This is Captain Carson of Company G, 23rd Missouri Cavalry, and Captain John Morgan, 3rd Arkansas Light Artillery. I have transferred them both, along with Company G and a section of the 3rd, to your command effective immediately."

Carson and Morgan rose from their seats. Morgan stuck out his hand with a broad grin. "Glad to meet you, Colonel."

Carson, also smiling, saluted O'Sullivan. There was something about that smile, and about the way he saluted, that O'Sullivan wasn't sure he liked.

"It's good to meet you, *Colonel*," Carson said. "The general has been filling us in on your... *remarkable* war record...."

"As I was saying, Captain Carson," Sherman said, with a slight edge to his voice, "Colonel O'Sullivan is a veteran of a half-dozen major campaigns in the west from Shiloh to Franklin and Nashville. He has my every confidence, and I expect both of you to defer to him in all things until this mess is over and done with. Is that clear?"

They nodded, but O'Sullivan was more than a little perturbed. There was no edge to Morgan; he was open and likeable. But there was something about Carsen he didn't like; he couldn't put his finger on it, but it was there. Carson was obviously old-school cavalry, probably West Point. His uniform was spotless, immaculately pressed, and had obviously been tailored to fit him precisely. His bearing, even when sitting, was upright, and his attitude was one of supreme confidence and... yes, arrogance. His somewhat thin face bore a haughty expression exaggerated by a classic Van Dyke beard and mustache that gave him an appearance that could, under certain conditions, be called demonic.

Hell, he's only missin' the bloody horns.

"Good," Sherman said, "then you can get to know each other when we're done here. Now, to the problem in hand. Colonel, I want White Eagle stopped. I want him either captured or dead. Either one will suit me just fine. If you can find him, and talk to him, you are to

100

offer him amnesty. These are the terms." He handed O'Sullivan an envelope.

"You can read it later. For now, I'll give you the short version. White Eagle must surrender himself and his chiefs into your custody. If he agrees, he and his people will be moved to a reservation in the eastern section of Colorado Territory. where they will be allowed to live in peace. There is no room for negotiation. He complies... or he dies; that's it. If he won't talk, he is to be taken by force and brought to trial for murder. I want these savages cleared out of the area, and I want it done quickly. Any questions?"

"An' just how quickly would that be, General?" O'Sullivan asked. "We don't even know where he is or what his strength might be."

"You have until the end of the year, Colonel. Five months. If it takes any longer than that, I'll want to know why."

"An' you said he'll be tried for murder," O'Sullivan said, quietly. "That's a hangin' offense. Did you really mean it, sir?"

"Absolutely, Colonel. He murdered two buffalo hunters, Jake Newsom, five civilian guards, and seven troopers at Newsom's Station, and he kidnapped a black woman. The son-of-a-bitch has been raidin' and killin' across the territory for months. The Santa Fe Trail has become a deathtrap. He has to be stopped, even it means wiping out every last one of 'em, women, children an' all. Goddamn savages. Understand?"

"I do, General."

"Colonel." Sherman looked thoughtfully at him. "I have every confidence in you, and in General Thomas' opinion of you and your abilities. *Do not* let us down."

O'Sullivan nodded. His face was a mask, expressionless. He turned and looked at Carson. The man's eyes were mere slits, and there was a slight smile on his lips.

"Very well, gentlemen, that's all I have for you. Colonel O'Sullivan, you leave at first light tomorrow morning. Make sure you have everything you need. I, too, am leaving tomorrow for Fort Zarah. If you need me, use the telegraph. Good luck, Colonel."

The three officers, O'Sullivan, Carson and Morgan, sat down together in the officer's dining area at Fort Larned to eat an early dinner. O'Sullivan intended to use the opportunity to get to know his new officers.

"Captain Carson, Captain Morgan," O'Sullivan said. "I'm glad to have you aboard, so I am, but I think it might be a good idea if we got to know each other before we head out tomorrow morning. Why don't you tell me a little about yourselves?" And then he leaned back in his chair to see who would go first.

Carson and Morgan looked at each, and then Morgan said, with a grin, "Might as well go first. John Morgan, Captain, graduated Virginia Military Institute in '58; third in my class of forty-eight. I studied artillery under Colonel Thomas Jackson, Stonewall Jackson, that is. When Virginia seceded, I did not. I stayed in the U.S. Army and served throughout the war, mostly in Virginia." His face took on a serious look as he continued, "I was at Bull Run, Antietam, Gettysburg and Yellow Tavern, and a few other places, before being sent out here in August last year. It was a busy war, but I never received a scratch. Lucky, I guess.... How about you, Captain Carson?"

Carson looked first at Morgan, then at O'Sullivan. "Well, unlike you, I did not see much action, I'm afraid. I was at Wilson's Creek in '61 and Pea Ridge in '62, but they hardly count, now do they?" he asked, dryly, looking pointedly at O'Sullivan. "I graduated West Point in '52 and spent the years before the war in Missouri; terribly boring time.

"Anyway, I was sent out here in January of '63 and have been fighting Indians ever since. General Sherman has probably made you aware of it, Capt... I mean Colonel... yes, I was at Sand Creek, and," he said, defiantly, "you can make of that what you will."

Morgan was dumfounded, not by the admission, but by the obvious lack of respect Carson had for O'Sullivan.

"Captain Morgan," O'Sullivan said, quietly, as he locked eyes with Carson. "Give us a moment, if you please."

Morgan stood. "I'll be outside the window, sir." He turned, walked to the door and left the building.

"Now then, you son-of-a-bitch," O'Sullivan said, quietly. His mouth was smiling; his eyes were not. "Let's have it. What's on your bloody mind?"

"Why, Colonel. I have no idea what you're talking about. I have nothing but respect for your... *rank*." He said it amiably enough, but there was an underlying edge to his voice.

"Not good enough, Captain. You obviously have something on your mind. I noticed it the first minute I met you in Sherman's office. We have to work together an' I'm damned if I'm gonna put up with a load of goddamn horseshit from you. If we can't work this out, I'm goin' right back to Sherman an' have you replaced. Now, what do you have to say for yourself?"

Carson's smile was gone, replaced by a look of grim determination. "You can do as you damned well please, *Colonel*. I earned my rank the hard way, and this damned command should have been mine. I earned that, too. My God, two years ago, you were nothing more than a sergeant major. Now look at you."

"You do have a problem, don't you, Captain? I can understand how you might feel but, by God, you're supposed to be a professional solder, an' an officer. What the hell did they teach you at the Point? Not to act like a bloody baby, of that I'm sure. Good enough, Captain." He pushed his chair back from the table and stood. "I will have you replaced. You may return to your quarters." Then he turned and walked toward the door.

"Wait. Colonel, a moment more, if you please, sir."

O'Sullivan returned to the table, stared down at him, and said, "Well, what is it?"

"You would ruin my career over this... this...."

"That I damned well would, Captain. You have shown that are not worthy of being a part of my command and, as such, I will not tolerate your lack of respect for my rank, earned or not, and for me as a person. Now, do you have anything else to say before I leave?"

Carson was silent for a long moment, then said, "You are right, Colonel. I was disrespectful and for that, I am truly sorry. It will not happen again. I respectfully request that you do not have me replaced and that I be allowed to remain in command of Company G."

"Sorry, is it? I bet you are at that, but you should learn to exercise some self-control, an' some bloody manners. Very well, Captain. You get one chance, and one chance only. One sideways look from you, one roll of the eyes, one slick remark, and you're gone. I have been in this man's army long enough to recognize you for exactly what you are, an' what you're capable of. I knew it the minute I laid eyes on you. People like you don't change, Carson. Cross me again and there'll be no more chances. Do you understand, Captain?"

Carson nodded and took a deep breath. "I do, Colonel. You have my word, sir."

"Very well, then. We'll say no more about it. From now on, this... incident never happened."

"Thank you, sir."

O'Sullivan nodded. Carson's words had been spoken with some feeling, but O'Sullivan had a deep-rooted feeling that this would not be the end of it. With an inaudible sigh, he turned in his seat, looked at the window, and beckoned. Morgan rejoined them just a moment later.

"We were talking about what happened at Sand Creek," O'Sullivan said, as Morgan sat down. "Did you know that Captain Carson was there?"

"I did, Colonel. The captain has made no secret of his feelings for the Indians. Very sad it was, what happened to his family."

Carson glared at Morgan. "I had not told the colonel about that, John."

"Then perhaps you should," O'Sullivan said. "I would like to know what happened, an'... well, one thing at a time. Please, Captain."

"My family, my wife, Loryanne, and my two little girls, Ann and Mary, were all killed by Cheyenne in September of '63. They were on their way to join me at Fort Zarah. The coach they were traveling in was attacked on the Santa Fe Trail twenty miles east of the fort; there were no survivors. My wife was scalped. My two girls... their throats were cut. I had to bury my family at Fort Zarah. So yes, Colonel," he said, quietly, looking O'Sullivan in the eye. "I was at Sand Creek, and yes, I did my share of the killing. Would have done more if I could, and with your permission, I will do more, much more. I'd like to see every last one of the stinking savages wiped off the face of the earth." He looked down at the tabletop, reached for his coffee, and took a small sip. Then he looked up at O'Sullivan, defiantly; his eyes were watering.

"O'Sullivan nodded. "Now I understand your bitterness, Captain, an', while I do also understand your need to for revenge, there will be none of it, not in my command. You cannot blame the many for the actions of a few. They are people, sir, and they are losing their lands, their food supply, and their heritage."

"I take it, then, Colonel, and I ask simply for clarification, that you do not agree with Washington's – and General Sherman's – mandate that the Indians be removed from the Great Plains?"

O'Sullivan thought for a moment, then said, "As an officer in the United States Army, I will do my duty to the best of my ability, regardless of what my conscience might tell me. I did not agree with the politics, on either side, which brought about the Civil War. Nor did I agree with many of the actions therein, or with the way many of them were carried out, including what happened to Georgia at the hands of General Sherman. As a soldier and patriot, however, I did my duty without question and without reservation, an' I will do so throughout this assignment. The Comanche *will* be moved to the Colorado Territory, and White Eagle will either go with them or he will be either killed or brought to justice."

Carson nodded, as did Morgan. It was a good answer to a tricky question.

"What of the general's orders that, if need be, the Indians be eradicated?" Morgan asked, looking at Carson as he said it.

"This is a war, Mr. Morgan. Not a war such as the one we have just fought and won, but a war nonetheless an' we shall do whatever it takes to win it. Now, that's enough of such things. We have much to discuss and much to get done before we leave in the morning. Is Company G ready to move out on an extended expedition, Captain Carson?"

"Absolutely, Colonel. General Sherman put us on notice two days ago, and we have drawn all the supplies and animals that we need for an extended campaign."

O'Sullivan nodded, and turned to Morgan. "What about you, Captain? You do realize that we'll be in the mountains? Are you prepared to move your guns across such terrain?"

"I am, Colonel. The mountain howitzer was designed for use in rough territory. We have a dozen pack mules as well as the artillery horses so, if need be, we can dismantle the guns and pack them up the mountains, or wherever else you might need to go. I have drawn fifty rounds of Hotchkiss, twenty-five of solid shot and one hundred canisters per gun along with sufficient powder for all. I consider that more than enough. Would you not agree, Colonel?"

O'Sullivan smiled. "I'm sure you learned your craft well, Captain. From what I have heard, General Jackson did not suffer fools lightly, especially when he was at the

Institute. The artillery is your department; I trust your judgement.

"Well, all appears to in order, then. I suggest we eat and then get an early night. It's sixty miles to Fort Dodge, and I would like to be there no later than mid-day on Wednesday. I suggest you have a good meal. It probably will the last you see in a good while. I will have a steak and potatoes. What will you order, gentlemen?"

Chapter 12

Bryson's Farm, Five Miles West of Ft. Aubry, August 7, Dusk

The Bryson family, Miles, Dora and their two small children, Kate age seven and Alice age five, had found the property they now called home in the late summer of 1863. Home it certainly was, comfortable it was... well, not so much. The farm, if you could call it that, was located five miles to the west of Fort Aubry on the south side of the Santa Fe Trail, on the north bank of the Arkansas River. It consisted of a low, two-room adobe shack, a small barn in serious need of repair, a small shed and a two-seater outhouse, all surrounded by a low rail fence, also in need of repair.

Miles and Dora Bryson were squatters, nice folks, but squatters just the same. They had happened upon the abandoned buildings while on their way west to Santa Fe in search of new life. What they were doing on the Mountain Branch of the Trail was anybody's guess, and without an escort, too, which is why they were able to stop off and take up residence in the old abandoned Eager Place. A big part of their decision to stay had been the farm's close proximity to Fort Aubry, and its location on the banks of the river, which meant there would never be a shortage of water.

Since their arrival in 1863, they had cleaned up the dwelling, repaired the roof, acquired two cows, which had produced two calves, and fifty or so chickens. They had brought with them two horses and a mule, and they had ploughed enough of the dirt-poor land to produce enough food, along with whatever meat Miles could shoot, to keep the family alive. Miles had even cobbled together a pump to transfer water from the river to house. It was a lonely and hard life they had chosen. They were dirt poor, but happy enough, safe in the knowledge that the military was less than five miles away.

It was dusk and the family was seated around a small table eating their evening meal when White Eagle, Yellow Crow, and three braves burst in through the door.

Miles Bryson started to rise, but was shot down by a blast from White Eagle's Sharps. The heavy ball slammed into his chest and hurled him backward into the fireplace.

Yellow Crow grabbed Dora while the three other warriors grabbed the two children. All three were dragged from the home. Miles was left lying in the fireplace, burning, but he felt no pain. He was already dead.

The raid on the Bryson farm lasted no more than fifteen minutes, during which time the cattle, horses, and mule were rounded up and driven off, the house and barn set afire, and Dora and the two children tied up and carried away. When the cavalry from Fort Aubry arrived at noon the following day, the Bryson farm was no more than smoking embers. Miles Bryson's body was not recovered.

White Eagle's Village, August 8

The ride from Bryson's farm to White Eagle's village took almost two days, more than seventy-five miles over some of the roughest mountain terrain in southeastern Colorado. By the time they arrived, it was already late afternoon and the women of the village were preparing the evening meal. All work stopped, however, when the war party rode into the village. Elders, women, children, and, of course, Elva, stopped what they doing, eager to see what their chief had brought back to them.

Dora Bryson was a striking young woman: tall, with blond hair that hung to her waist — something the Comanche in the village had never seen before. They stared at her in wonder as she slid down from the back of Yellow Crow's pony. The two children, Kate and Alice, also blondes, had long since given up crying, but their faces were tear-stained and streaked with dirt, dust thrown up from the pony's hooves over the long ride. Elva, knowing how the family must be feeling, rushed over to them, wrapped her arm around Dora's shoulder, and gathered the two children to her skirts.

Yellow Crow, seeing Elva run to Dora, leaped down from the pony's back, his face drawn tight with rage. He grabbed Elva by the hair and pulled her away, throwing her roughly to the ground, shouting something she didn't understand.

White Eagle also saw Elva run to Dora and the children, and Yellow Crow's treatment of her. In a trice,

112

he was down from his pony and had run the twenty yards to where Yellow Crow was still standing over her, shouting. Almost without stopping, the chief slammed into him, knocking him to the ground. For a moment, Yellow Crow lay still, momentarily stunned by the sudden attack. White Eagle stood over him, legs apart, fists clenched at his side, and waited. Yellow Crow looked up at him, saw the anger on his face, and bowed his head in submission. White Eagle nodded, then turned and took Elva by the arm and helped her to her feet.

"You... take them," he gestured toward Dora and the children, "there." This time he waved his hand toward the teepee next to his own, and he looked again at Yellow Crow, his intent was unmistakable.

"Come with me," Elva said to Dora, taking her hand. "Keep your head up. These people admire courage and despise weakness. Do what I tell you, and you'll be well treated. Come."

Elva lifted the flap and entered the teepee. It was little different from the one she now called home, though she had no other choice. The fire pit was clean, free of ashes. There were a few skins in a small pile, but obviously not enough – the nights were cold in the mountains, and Dora would need more to keep the children warm.

"Wait here for me. Do not go outside. I'll be back in a minute," Elva instructed.

She returned a few moments later, dragging a huge bundle of buffalo skins. "Here, help me with these. You'll have something to sleep on."

"Who... who are you? They killed my husband and... what will they do to us?"

"I'm Elva, and I don't know. I've been here only two weeks myself. I don't think they intend to hurt you. They haven't hurt me – and no, no, they haven't... touched me, not yet, anyway. White Eagle seems to have made me his woman, but he has not taken me to his bed."

"They killed my husband, burned our farm...." Dora burst into tears, which caused Alice and Kate to wail loudly.

"Stop it! Stop it NOW! I told you. They will not tolerate weakness. There's nothing you can do, nothing. You have to be strong, all of you, especially you... for the sake of the children. What is your name?"

"Dora, it's Dora," she gasped, between sobs.

"You have to be strong. Hold your head up. Stand up straight. Clean your face, and the children's. Here, let me." Elva wiped the tears from the children's faces with the hem of her shirt.

"When White Eagle comes to you, stand up and face him. Look him in the eye. Do not speak unless he speaks to you. Do not cry; do not beg. And do what he asks immediately and without question."

No sooner had she said it than the flap was flung back and the chief entered. Elva stood to one side. Dora took a step back, placed herself between White Eagle and her children, and did as Elva had told her. She drew herself up to her full height, put her shoulders back, and stared the Comanche in the eye.

For a moment, he stood in front of her, staring at her. The black war paint was gone, but his face was stern and haughty. Then the corners of his mouth turned upward in the beginnings of a smile, and he turned to Elva and said, "This woman... this children. You take care of them."

Elva dipped her head in assent.

"It is good," he said to Dora. "We not hurt you, children. You be good; do what you told. No harm come you."

He looked around the interior of the teepee, saw the pile of skins Elva had brought in. "Blankets. Children need blankets. All need...." He reach out and touched Elva's shirt, and then her skirt, his eyebrows raised in a silent question.

"Clothes. You mean clothes."

He nodded, and smiled a little. "Clothes, good."

"Please," Dora said, to Elva, "ask him what is to become of us."

Elva smiled at her. "It is best that you talk to him yourself. He speaks some English, and he understands it quite well. Tell him your name, and those of the children, then ask him. He will tell you."

"But he murdered my husband." Her face was taut, her voice defiant.

"Yes, and there's nothing you can do about it. If you fight him, you will lose, and so," she looked at Kate and Alice, "will the children. You have to submit. There's no other choice. If you can't, you must pretend to, at least for now. Talk to him. Do not show weakness."

White Eagle listened to the conversation between the two women. He looked at Elva, his eyes narrowed in concentration, then he looked at Dora and waited.

She drew herself up to her full height, put her shoulders back, took a deep breath, tilted her head back slightly, looked him in the eye, and said, "My name is Dora–"

"Dora," he interrupted her. "White Eagle," he said, placing his hand on his chest.

"And... and, this is Alice, and Kate."

He nodded, his face softening.

"You killed my husband. What will you do to me?"

"Do? Nothing. You stay here, in village. Good life for woman. You safe. Comanche not harm you.

"You," he said to Elva. "They need fire, food, you show." Then he turned a walked out through the flap.

That night, their first as captives, though they were warm and well fed, Dora and her children slept little. For Elva, that night was the first that White Eagle took her to his bed.

Chapter 13

They rode into Fort Dodge a little before one o'clock in the afternoon on Wednesday. Captain Pearce, Lieutenants Daly and Warwick, along with Sergeant Major Boone Coffin were waiting on the open porch of the new command office. They all looked at O'Sullivan in amazement when they saw the new rank on his shoulders.

"Congratulations, *Colonel*, sir," Daly said from the porch as O'Sullivan and his new retinue of officers dismounted and tied their horses to the rail.

Coffin said nothing. He simply smiled, enigmatically, down upon the group, who soon joined them on the porch.

"Thank you, Lieutenant," O'Sullivan said, a little self-consciously. "Captain Pearce; do you have room in your office where we can talk? I need to explain what's going on."

"It'll be tight, Colonel," Pearce almost choked as he called O'Sullivan by his new rank, "but we can make it work, I'm sure." He paused, then said, "Um, Colonel, am I to assume from your new rank that you are taking over command here at Fort Dodge?"

"Not at all, Captain. I have an agenda all my own, so I do, as I'll explain when we are inside," he said, brushing past and through the office door.

Pearce was right; it was tight inside his office, even though it had been built with a larger purpose in mind.

"Gentlemen," O'Sullivan began. "First I will introduce you to your new comrades in arms. On the left are the officers and company sergeant major of my own Company K. First Lieutenant Glendon Daly, Second Lieutenant Dillman Warwick, and Sergeant Major Boone Coffin, who will from now on act as sergeant major for both companies.

"Captain Pearce, for you new men, is the officer commanding the construction of Fort Dodge. On the right are Captains Hamilton Carson, commanding Company G, 23rd Missouri Cavalry, and Captain John Morgan, 3rd Arkansas Light Artillery. Also on the right is First Lieutenant Ewan Keogh, and with a name like that," he said, with a smile, "you'll know that he can only be a fellow a countryman of mine. Finally, there's Second Lieutenant Charles Whitworth. We don't have time for everyone to get to know each other right now. That will have to come later."

Keogh was not impressed. He looked first at O'Sullivan, then at Carson. The look they exchanged was one of mutual understanding, and Coffin didn't miss it.

Keogh was a diminutive individual, made to look even smaller by the huge black beard that covered more than half of his face. The beard hid most of the livid red scar that ran under it from the right corner of his mouth

118

to a point just below the center of his right eye. The man looked more pirate than cavalry officer.

"For now, gentlemen," O'Sullivan continued, "all you need to know is our assignment—"

"Colonel," Pearce interrupted him, "before you go into details, you should know that there's been another attack, two days ago." He walked around the desk to face the map on the wall, and pointed. "Here, about five miles west of Fort Aubry. The Bryson farm was hit late yesterday. Bryson is dead; there's no sign of the wife or children. All of the animals are gone, too."

"Are we sure it was White Eagle?"

"No, we're not. Whoever it was left little sign. But who else could it be?"

"Cheyenne, Arapaho?" O'Sullivan asked, of no one in particular.

"I don't think so," Daly said, shaking his head, thoughtfully. "Fort Aubry is too far south for them. They are located mostly to the north and west of Great Bend. They wouldn't come this far. No.... I'd say it's White Eagle."

"He's right," Carson said. "They would not travel this far out."

"Hmmm...." O'Sullivan stared at the map, his right elbow in his left hand, his chin cupped in his right hand. "How far is it from here to Fort Aubry... and Fort Lyon?"

119

"Fort Aubry is three day's ride from here. With wagons and artillery, it's more like four days," Pierce said. "Fort Lyon is sixty miles farther to the west, say another two days, at least. In all, probably six to seven days, if you don't stop for anything other than overnight."

"Thank you, Captain Pearce," O'Sullivan said. "Well, just so that everyone here knows, our job is to find White Eagle and persuade him to surrender. Finding him is not going to be easy; gettin' him to surrender.... You're the Indian fighter, Lieutenant Daly. What are the chances of that happening, do you think?"

Daly shook his head. "Little to none, Colonel."

Captain Carson?"

"I'd put the chances of that animal giving himself up at less than zero. He will fight to the death."

O'Sullivan nodded. "I can't say I disagree with either of you, but," he looked hard at Carson, "we have to give it our best try. But where do we start?" It was more of an observation than a question, and O'Sullivan was not expecting a reply. "Before I left for Fort Larned, we had decided on Fort Lyon. Now, however, we have this incident at Fort Aubry to consider. Your thoughts, gentlemen? By the way, do you two know each other?" He looked at Carson, and then at Daly.

"Oh yes, we know each other, and I know Lieutenant Keogh," Daly said, with a tight smile. "We were all at Sand Creek together. How are you, Captain, Lieutenant?"

"Well enough, I suppose," Carson said, with a dark look.

Keogh said nothing; he simply stared at Daly, his dark eyes glittering.

O'Sullivan could tell there was obvious friction between the three men, but now was not the time to find out about it. That would have to be done later, and in private.

"Fort Aubry or Fort Lyon, then?" O'Sullivan asked.

"There's little to be learned at what's left at the Bryson farm," Pearce said, "I suggest you stick to the original plan. Er... sorry, Colonel. None of my business."

"That's all right, Captain, your input is always welcome, and I'm inclined to agree with you." O'Sullivan stepped up to the map. "This new incident only confirms what we already know – think – that his camp, village, whatever it is, must be somewhere in this area, here." He swept his hand over a large, seemingly blank area of the map. "An' this area, so Lieutenant Daly tells me, is nothing but mountains threaded through by the Arkansas and Smoky Hill Fork rivers an' several branches thereof. It makes sense then that he would be hiding somewhere here, where there's plenty of water. It's possible there are as many as three hundred of 'em. Who is in command at Fort Aubry, Captain Pearce?"

"Fort Aubry is something of an anomaly, Colonel. It's not a fort at all, at least not yet. It's more of a way station. For more than ten years, it was simply a military camp without a name. Early in '64, it was named Camp

Wynkoop, to honor Fort Lyon's commander. No sooner was it officially named than the army abandoned it, leaving the way station to fend for itself. Now, as of only a month ago, the army is back again. Two companies of the 48th Wisconsin Infantry under the command of Lieutenant Colonel Henry Shears arrived there late last month to begin building a new army outpost. As of right now, there's little there other than a bunch of infantry housed in tents. Fort Lyon would be your best option, if I may say so, Colonel."

"An' I assume that Lieutenant Colonel Wynkoop is in command at Fort Lyon," O'Sullivan replied.

"Yes, and no. Colonel Wynkoop is indeed at Fort Lyon but, so I understand, he is there only to investigate the Sand Creek affair, and Colonel Chivington in particular." Pearce paused and looked at Carson and Keogh, who were now decidedly uncomfortable. "I assume that Major Scott Anthony is still in command fort. He certainly was when Colonel Wynkoop was transferred to Fort Riley a couple of days before the massacre. Anyway, both of them are there now."

"Fort Lyon it is, then," O'Sullivan decided. "We'll stop by Fort Aubry on the way, see if Colonel Shears has anything to add. We'll take two days here to prepare, if you agree, Captain Pearce."

"Of course. If there's anything you need, supplies, animals, just let me know. I'll let you have what I can. In the meantime, Colonel, I'd like to invite you to dinner this evening. We've killed another steer. The steaks are on me."

O'Sullivan grinned at the memory of another time gone by. "Make mine big an' rare, Captain."

Later that same afternoon, in the confines of his tent, O'Sullivan sat down with Boone Coffin to talk. He was not at all happy to have learned all that he now had about the fiasco at Sand Creek, and Coffin was the one person in the world he trusted without reservation.

"So, Boone," he said.

"So, *Colonel*," Coffin said, with a huge grin.

"Eh, it's temporary, brevet rank, so it is. Back to captain when this mess is over an' done with." O'Sullivan's Irish brogue was stronger now that they talking informally. "Look you, Boone, this is not what I was bargaining' for, not at all. I knew I had a problem with Carson, an' I knew it before I left Fort Larned, but I didn't know to what extent, an' Keogh; well, I had no idea at all. I had a run in with Carson the night before we moved out. Almost replaced him, but I let him talk me out of it, so I did. Now I'm wonderin' if I done the right thing."

"They're a couple of bad ones, if ever I saw such. We've known a few like 'em, that's for sure. I'll keep a sharp eye on them, Ronan. If I see a twitch I don't like, I'll tell you about it. Can't do much more than that."

O'Sullivan nodded his agreement. "Let's get Daly in here. He was with 'em at Sand Creek."

Coffin nodded, rose to his feet, and ducked out under the flap. He was back minutes later with Lieutenant Daly.

"Lieutenant Daly, how are you? Take a seat, both of you," O'Sullivan invited.

"I'm well... Colonel. Congratulations on your promotion."

"As I told the sergeant major, it's temporary, a brevet rank: all responsibility and no extra pay for it. What do they call you for short, Lieutenant, Glendon or Glen?"

"Glen will do fine, Colonel."

"Yes, well, only when we're in private," O'Sullivan said, reaching for his coffee mug. Finding it empty, he handed it to Coffin, his eyebrows raised in request. Coffin nodded, took the mug, and left the tent.

"Glen," O'Sullivan said, looking the man squarely in the eye. "I want to know about Carson and Keogh. Tell it like it is. Nothing you say to me will leave this tent, but I have to know what I'm dealing with."

Daly nodded and took a deep breath. "You're gonna need to watch those two. If you remember, I mentioned that there were officers who insisted that we chase the survivors down an' kill them. Carson an' Keogh were two of those officers."

Coffin reappeared, bearing three mugs of steaming coffee. O'Sullivan took his, and then waited until the other two men were settled.

"Go on, Lieutenant."

"Well, as I said. I arrived a little late to the party, thank God. I'd have been court marshalled for insubordination if not. Anyway, the Indians were camped along the west bank of the creek. The area, mostly grasslands, was flat, an' muddy. Chivington attacked from the west. The Indians didn't know what hit 'em, so I'm told. The whole thing didn't last but a few minutes. The troopers rode back and forth through the village, firing at anything that moved. They call it a battle; it was no such thing.

"As I said, when we got there a few minutes later. Chivington was riding around shouting at the officers. Carson an' Keogh had dismounted an', along with several troopers, were going teepee to teepee. Those two are close, Colonel, real close. Keogh was excited. He had a knife in his hand, an' his tunic an' face were splashed with blood. I saw him haul one young woman out of a teepee an' cut her throat. He slashed at her like a wild thing, then threw her down and rushed back into the teepee. He was in there but a moment then came out waving a hunk of hair in the air, a scalp.

"Carson was more methodical, cold an' deliberate. He want from one teepee to the next. He'd fling back the flap, look inside, let go with his pistol, then walk on to the next one. I'd say, that between 'em, they must have killed a dozen, maybe more.

"When Chivington called a halt to the carnage, Carson an' Keogh mounted an' made as if to go chasing what few survivors there were into the mountains, but the colonel was having none of it. I saw 'em shouting back an' forth, but was too far away to hear it all. Carson was mighty angry though. I heard later, from one of Chivington's staff officers, that he was insisting that they go get the rest of the goddamn savages, that he wouldn't rest until every last one of 'em had gone to hell." He took a sip of his coffee, looked first at O'Sullivan, then at Coffin, then shook his head, shrugged his shoulders, and rose to his feet. "Please excuse me, Colonel," he said and left the tent.

It was a long moment before O'Sullivan spoke. "Bejesus, Boone. What in the name of the Holy Mother have we gotten into?"

Coffin merely looked at him; he knew it was a rhetorical question, and that it required no answer.

"Boone, if what Daly says is true, an' I see no reason to doubt it, we have a couple of maniacs on our hands. Carson told me himself that his family had been wiped out by Cheyenne in '63, an' that he had vowed to make 'em pay for it. Seems he wasn't lyin'. I told him I was havin' none of it, but... well, I guess we'll have to wait an' see.

"He also made it very clear that he had expected to be given this command, an' that he had no time at all for me. How the hell he knew I had just been promoted is beyond me. Sherman made a point of me wearin' the rank patches before he introduced me to Carson; an' I know he did that for good reason. But the man knew, told me as much, so he did."

The two men sat quietly, sipping on their coffee. Then Coffin said, "From what Lieutenant Daly said, they are as bad as one another. They could be dangerous, Ronan. Better watch your back, especially at night. It's not unknown for... well, you know."

"Yeah, unfortunately, I know only too well. Remember what happened to Sergeant Frye at Stones River? They never did find out who did that."

Coffin nodded. "Yeah, well. It happens more often that you'd think. In the meantime, we need to watch 'em both, an', as I said, I'll watch your back."

O'Sullivan nodded thoughtfully.

Chapter 14

Santa Fe Trail, August 12

They left Fort Dodge at ten o'clock on Saturday morning. Now that the two companies of cavalry had combined, they were an impressive sight. A column of threes stretched for more than a quarter mile, with four wagons, a full section of artillery, and eighteen pack mules. They filed slowly out of Fort Dodge and onto the Santa Fe Trail, heading west toward Cimarron and the Mountain Branch of the Trail.

At the head of the column, Lieutenant Colonel Ignatius O'Sullivan was accompanied by Captain Carson, Captain Morgan, First Lieutenant Daly, and Sergeant Major Boone Coffin. First Lieutenant Keogh was at the head of Company G. Second Lieutenant Warwick was farther toward the rear of the column at the head of Company K.

For the first several miles, they rode together in silence. There was now no denying the friction between O'Sullivan and Carson, though both of them kept it well in check.

By nightfall, they had reached the ruins of what had been Fort Atkinson, a U.S. Army outpost long abandoned. Dreary though it was the foundations of its adobe buildings now little more than markers for what once had been. It seemed a good place to camp for the night.

Seated together around the campfire, all seven officers and Coffin were eating bacon, beans and bread washed down with thick black coffee. The night sky, but for a few fast-moving white clouds, was clear with a full moon set among a glittering field of stars. To the west, the skyline rose, jet-black and undulating – stark monsters of the night that seemed to twist and turn as the scudding clouds briefly obscured the moonlight that glistened on the peaks and ridges.

The night air was hot, and the men, officers included, were stripped down to their shirts and britches. The hour was late, almost midnight, and, but for the crackle of the campfire, all was quiet, except.... Somewhere, far away across the grasslands, a coyote howled its mournful call, and was answered a moment later by another, seemingly miles away in the opposite direction.

The company and the conversation would have been pleasant, had it not been for the underlying tension among the assembled officers. Somehow, they had managed to seat themselves around the fire in two separate factions. Carson and Keogh. And O'Sullivan, Coffin, Daly, Warwick and Whitworth. They had been seated there for several hours; the rest of men long since bedded down for the night.

"So, Cap... Colonel," Carson appeared to stumble on the words.

O'Sullivan looked sharply at him, his mouth a tight, thin line, but he said nothing.

"You were at the battle of Franklin, so I understand."

O'Sullivan nodded.

"Quite the slaughterhouse, was it not? The Rebs were virtually leaderless, yes? Simply charged into the guns, so I'm told. It must have been like shootin' fish in a barrel." The words were innocent enough, but they had an underlying hint of contempt, and all present were aware of it.

Keogh smiled and stared across the flickering embers at O'Sullivan.

"What are you implying, Captain?" O'Sullivan asked.

"Why nothing, nothing at all, Colonel. Just trying to make conversation, is all."

For a long moment, O'Sullivan stared at him. "I know what you're up to, Carson, an' I'll humor you. You want to know what it was like at Franklin? But you were at Pea Ridge, so you should know all about such things, right? After all, that was major battle; lasted all of four hours, did it not? An' what, three thousand casualties in all? I saw more men die in the space of a half-hour at Franklin, so I did."

The sarcasm was plain for all to hear, and he was exaggerating, a little, but everyone seated there knew that Pea Ridge, when compared to the Battle of Franklin, was little more than an isolated skirmish.

"Well, I'll tell you," O'Sullivan continued. "More men died at Franklin in the space of a half-hour than at Pea Ridge an' Wilson's Creek combined. Every officer below the rank of colonel, in my regiment alone, was either killed or wounded. We suffered almost fifty percent casualties. An' the Rebs, as you called 'em.... Fine men, officers an' soldiers, each an' every last one of 'em, they were. Six Confederate generals died that day at the front of their brigades an' divisions. No Carson, they weren't leaderless, though their commanding general must have been out of his mind, as must have been Colonel Chivington that day at Sand Creek." He looked pointedly, first at Keogh and then Carson.

Keogh choked into his coffee mug. Carson merely smiled at him, and slowly nodded his head.

"Maybe not out of his mind," Carson said, quietly. "More like a man on a mission, at least that was my impression. As was I," he added, defiantly.

Coffin leaned forward a little, trying to look at Carson around the flames. "Captain, just how many did you, yourself, account for that day?" It was a loaded question, and one Coffin was sure he wouldn't answer.

"Not sure. I didn't count. I was just thinking about killing as many savages as I could. Eight, I think, maybe nine. Keogh, here, did better than I, though I think his motives were different from mine, right, Ewan?"

Even by the light of the fire, it was easy to see that Keogh's face had taken on an angry hue.

"What goddamn business is it of yours, Sergeant Major?" Keogh was so angry he could barely get the words out. "An' what the hell are you, a goddamn non-com, doing sittin' here with the officers?"

Coffin was about to answer, but he didn't get a chance.

"I'll tell you the answer to both questions, *Lieutenant*," O'Sullivan snapped. "He's here because I invited him. Wherever I go, he goes. Second, he's responsible for the good order of this command. And the good attitude of its officers, you included, is paramount to that good order. I know what you are, Keogh, and so does everyone sitting here. You would have enjoyed the war, the killin', so you would, so long as those you were killin' were defenseless, like those poor kids at Sand Creek."

With the exception of Carson, Keogh, Coffin and O'Sullivan, the rest of the officers were uneasy, tense and ill at ease at the unprecedented exchange they were witnessing.

"You're a nasty little bastard, Keogh," O'Sullivan continued. "A stone killer, cold an' remorseless, but not here, not in this command. You pull any of that stuff you pulled at Sand Creek an' I'll kill you m'self.

"You, Carson," he turned his head to look at him, and calmly said, "I've met men like you before, so I have, a great many of 'em. You're lookin' for revenge, an' I can't say I blame you; been down that trail m'self, and only a couple of months ago. But here's the thing, an'

132

I've seen it too many times. Most people, those with a conscience, that is, almost always do somethin' they live to regret, but they always... always will justify what they do, by any means they can, an' the sad thing is they believe their own horseshit, but it's never good enough, so it isn't. Killin' for the sake of it is... well, it's a sickness that will eventually destroy you.

"You're right, Captain Carson. I'm a sergeant major in heart an' mind, an' a bloody good one, even if I do say so m'self. But right now I'm a lieutenant colonel in the United States Army, an' whether you like it or not, I'm your commandin' officer. How the hell I let you talk me into keepin' you in this command is beyond me. But hear this, Carson. The same goes for you as for half-pint, there." He nodded in the direction of Keogh. "You step out of line just an inch, either one of you, an' I'll drop you where you stand. May the Holy Mother strike me down if I don't.

"Now then, gentlemen," he said, lightly, as he rose to his feet. "I suggest we go get some sleep, before this friendly little chat turns into somethin' we'll all regret. I wish you all good night." And with that, he turned, and without a backward look, and walked swiftly to his tent.

For a long moment, the rest of the group sat looking at one another, not knowing quite what to say or what to do next.

Carson sat still, thoughtfully stroking his Van Dyke. There was a tight, enigmatic smile on his face, but his eyes were without humor, mere slits in a face whose

133

gaunt lines were accentuated by the shadows, stark in the dying light from the campfire. Keogh was visibly enraged, and would have rose had not Carson put hand on his arm and restrained him, "Later!" he muttered, so that he could be heard only by Keogh.

Coffin was totally relaxed. He was seated on the ground, leaning back on his elbows, smiling broadly. Daly, Morgan, Warwick and Whitworth were dumbfounded by what had happened. Never had any of them, even Warwick, experienced anything like it before, and he had, himself in the past, felt O'Sullivan's ire.

"You've made yourself an enemy, two of 'em, in fact," Coffin said, a few minutes later when he dipped under the flap and into O'Sullivan's tent.

"Nah, Carson became my enemy even before I met him, as soon as he found out he wasn't getting the command. I should have left both of 'em back at Fort Larned, so I should."

At the same time Coffin was talking to O'Sullivan, Carson and Keogh, now in the relative seclusion of Carson's, tent, were also discussing the events of the past hour.

"I'm gonna kill 'im," Keogh spluttered, angrily. "The no account son of a bitch will get his just as soon as...."

"Not now, Ewan," Carson interrupted him. "This is not the place for such talk."

"But...."

"Not now, I said. There will be plenty of time, and opportunity. Fear not. I am, after all, the senior captain here, right?" He said it quietly, but with an edge to his voice that was unmistakable in its intent.

The command rose early the following morning, the thirteenth. It was Sunday, but somehow that fact by-passed them all; there were no prayers or devotions. Instead, the men went about their daily routines. They concentrated first on breakfast, and then they readied themselves for whatever might lie ahead. Carson and Keogh were uncharacteristically quiet that morning. Not so O'Sullivan. He emerged from his tent well rested, in good humor, and not in the least perturbed by the memories of what had occurred only a few hours earlier.

By nine o'clock that morning, they were back on the road and heading west toward Fort Aubry.

Chapter 15

Fort Lyon, August 17

It took three more days for O'Sullivan's column to reach Fort Aubry. Captain Pearce had been right in his assumption that the fort was far from complete. There was little room and no accommodation available for the large number of troops that made up the command. After an overnight stay under canvas, and a pleasant evening with Lieutenant Colonel Shears, O'Sullivan headed west to Fort Lyon. They passed by the sad remains of what once had been the Bryson farm, but they didn't stop. There was nothing left to see, only ashes. They arrived late in the afternoon of Thursday, August 17, tired, dusty, and irritable.

They were expected. Major Anthony had left a message with the guard that he was to be informed as soon as the column arrived. When he received word that the column had been spotted still some distance away, he sent word to Colonel Wynkoop that they would be arriving within the hour. He also had rooms prepared for the officers, and meals prepared for all.

At O'Sullivan's request, he, Colonel Wynkoop, and Major Anthony dined alone that evening. He was determined to get an unbiased opinion about the Indian situation, and he wanted to learn all he could about Carson and Keogh.

Anthony was a heavy-set, hearty individual; Wynkoop was not at all what he had expected. Tall, slim, black wavy hair, clean-shaven except for a Mexican-style mustache, and a black silk cravat tied in a bow at his throat, all of which gave him the appearance of a dashing corsair, rather than the serious infantry commander O'Sullivan knew him to be.

The meeting was friendly. The early conversation inevitably turned to the recent war and their experience, but soon turned to the problems in hand, in which Colonel Wynkoop was still very much involved.

"Sand Creek, Colonel," Wynkoop leaned forward and placed his folded arms on the table, "was partially my fault. No, I had no hand in it, wasn't even there. I had been posted to Fort Riley two days earlier, on the twenty-seventh. Chivington was left in command, though how the hell that happened I have no idea. His commission had expired two weeks earlier. Technically, he wasn't even in the army.

"The Cheyenne and the Arapaho were at Sand Creek because I sent them there. I was in command here, at Fort Lyon, and I negotiated a peace agreement with Black Kettle and persuaded him to take his people to the Creek where they would be under my protection. I also advised him to fly the American flag over his village so there would be no doubt that his intentions were friendly, and he did so.

"I received orders to report to Fort Riley, and left this place on the twenty-seventh. Chivington arrived here later that day and, finding me gone, decided to take action against Black Kettle. The results, you already know. The man murdered countless defenseless souls, most of them women and children. My job now is to investigate the massacre, and Colonel Chivington, and see that justice is done, though I doubt very much that he will be made to answer for his crime, what with the attitude in Congress, and the Army High Command."

"Where is he now, Chivington?" O'Sullivan asked.

"Gone home to Nebraska, so I'm told." Wynkoop shrugged.

"And the rest of his officers? What of them?"

Some are still here... two, so I understand, you have with you."

"That would seem to be the case, so it would. Captain Hamilton Carson and Lieutenant Ewan Keogh. What do you know of them, if you don't mind me askin'?"

"Not at all." Wynkoop thought for a moment, considering what he was about to say. "Keogh... he's... he's a killer; no other words for it. From the reports I already have, the man was maniacal: ran from teepee to teepee, killing whatever moved, laughing, covered in blood. I'm told he killed at least ten, took scalps, too, among other things." Wynkoop lowered and shook his head, and stared down at the tabletop, seemingly lost in thought.

Carson is different," he said, looking up. He leaned back in his chair. "He doesn't drink; at least, he didn't –

most of Chivington's men got drunk the night before the attack, so you can imagine…. Carson, he's cold, and he's driven. Yes, I know what happened to his family, and I suppose I can understand his need for revenge, but…."

O'Sullivan nodded. "I know what you're tryin' to say, Colonel. I've had a couple of run-ins with him m'self, an' the man is hard to read, so he is. Major Anthony?"

Anthony nodded in agreement. "Yes, I've known Carson a long time, before his family was killed. He was different then: a good man, good officer, now… well, he's cold, as you say, Colonel Wynkoop, and bitter. Keogh, whew; that man is… evil is the only word I can think of to describe him. He's sly too, and a liar. I'd watch yourself when you're around him, Colonel. I have no doubt he would shoot a man in the back, if he thought he could get away it."

The three men sat in silence, sipping on their coffee, then Wynkoop looked up at O'Sullivan. "Let's go to my office. We can discuss your plans there. You, too, Major. Your input will be valuable."

Just a few minutes later they were all three seated in front of Wynkoop's desk. The wall at the rear was covered by a huge, topographical map showing southeastern Colorado, western Kansas, and Indian Territory to the south.

"All right, Mr. O'Sullivan, let's hear it,"

O'Sullivan stood and walked to the map; he was now well familiar with the territory.

139

"I've given it a lot of thought over the past several weeks, so I have. We're here." He pointed to the spot on the map. "He hit Fort Dodge here, the buffalo camp here, and the Bryson farm here. He also hit Newsom's Station just down the road from here. The timing of all of those attacks was over a period of just five weeks, give or take a few days. We know for sure where he ain't. He ain't down here." He swept the palm of his hand over a wide area to the south of the Mountain Branch of the Santa Fe Trail. "An' that means his village has to be up in these mountains... somewhere here." Again, he swept his hand over the map. "An' that, so I understand, is some rough country, yes, Major?"

"That it is, Colonel. Some of those peaks rise to more than twelve thousand feet. Getting wagons and artillery up there will be all but impossible."

"Yeah, we'll have to pack it most of the way, I think."

Wynkoop nodded, "Where will you start? Do you have any ideas, Colonel?"

"There's only one place to start: right here," O'Sullivan pointed to a specific spot on the map, almost due west from Fort Lyon. "As I said, the timing of his attacks is important; he can travel only so far in a day; he has to be somewhere in that area; has to be."

He turned away from the map, and looked at them; they were both nodding their agreement.

"The thing is, gentlemen," O'Sullivan said, "how the hell do I get there? Any ideas, Major, Colonel?"

They looked at each other.

"I do, Colonel, but it won't be easy." Anderson stood and went to the map. "Here, just to the south of Newsom's Station, is an arroyo, a dry riverbed. Been dry for years as long as I've been up here. Might see a trickle when it rains, but that's about all. Mostly it's been used by hunters and prospectors as a trail into the mountains. I've patrolled it several times, as Colonel Wynkoop knows, it's pretty rough; there's no room for wagons once you leave the Santa Fe, but it's passable for horses and mules. It winds through the foothills for several miles, maybe eight or ten, rising only slightly, then it heads sharply upward for several miles more until it splits, not just once but, over a distance of maybe two miles, at least a dozen times into smaller, much narrower trails. Where they lead to is anybody's guess. I've explored a couple of them. They all seem to head westward and upward. And, Colonel, it's ideal country for bushwhackers and ambush. You could lose your entire command up there."

"Is that so?" O'Sullivan stared up at the map, at the area Anthony had been describing. "Gotta start somewhere. That's as good a place as any, I s'pose." He looked at Anderson, and said, "Do you have any scouts that know that area?"

"I think the one you have with you, Bear Claw, isn't it? He probably knows the area as well as any. He's Shoshone. I know him. He's a good man, loyal. The

141

Apaches, I don't know. I can let you have a couple more, if you like, but I think Bear Claw is your best bet."

Wynkoop pulled his pocket watch from his vest pocket, flipped it open, and noted the time. "It's getting late, gentlemen. Time we hit the sack. I have a lot to do tomorrow, and so, Colonel, do you. When do you plan on leaving?"

"I need at least a couple of days to prepare, if that's all right with you, Major Anthony."

"Of course. Take all the time you need. You have a room at your disposal; I can see that your animals are fed. Your men will have to fend for themselves, but that shouldn't be a problem."

"In that case, I plan to leave here on the morning of the twentieth." He rose and offered his hand to each man in turn, thanked them for their help and hospitality, returned their salutes, and went to his room, where he found Coffin waiting for him.

"You were right, old son," O'Sullivan said. "Keogh is the man to watch. From what I've heard, he's not beyond puttin' a ball in man's back, an' where we're goin', well, you just watch me back, an' I'll watch yours. We'll be here for the next couple o' days, then it's off up into the mountains we'll be. I've a feelin' things might just come to a head. You stay close, you hear? You take orders from no one but me, an' that goes especially for Carson an' Keogh."

"Gotcha. What about Morgan an' Whitworth?"

"Morgan's old school, will toe the line an' do what's required. Whitworth, the same, though he lacks any experience at all. Boone, I want you to keep your ears open. Any signs o' troublemaking, I want to know about it, officers or men, especially while we're here an' everyone's in close quarters, so to speak."

"Sure, though most of 'em know we're close, you an' me, so they'll be watchin' their tongues, that's for sure."

"Yep, they will, but you have a knack o' bein' able to read a man, Boone, an' the situation, always have. That's why you, both of us, survived the war. I wouldn't have made it through without you, so I wouldn't. So let's not falter now. We have a couple o' bad uns, here, an' they worry me, so they do."

Coffin nodded. "You can count on me, Ronan."

Chapter 16

Robbin's Hole, August 20

Robbin's Hole, a small way station at the confluence of the Purgatoire River and the Santa Fe Trail, was located some twenty miles to the northeast of Trinidad. It was a busy station, at times, a stopover for stagecoaches and wagon trains. The main building was a huge, two-and-a-half story log structure that housed a dining area, kitchen, a saloon of sorts. A general store was located on the ground floor, guest bedrooms on the upper floor, and Will Robbin's own living quarters in the attic.

Mornings and evenings, when the stagecoaches arrived and left, were always busy but the hours between ten in the morning and three in the afternoon were mostly quiet times. One minute, the station was a bustling hive of activity, the next it seemed to be almost deserted. It was those quiet hours, after the overnight crowd had left, that the staff, just Will and his four male helpers, cleaned up the place. It was also the time when the saloon was occupied only be the odd drifter who happened by.

In addition to his four helpers, Will also employed four guards, though he didn't pay them himself; the stagecoach companies did.

And so it was that around noon that hot day in late August, Will Robbin and his people were going about their daily tasks. Will was restocking the shelves in the store, Jed was behind the bar in the saloon, keeping two strangers well supplied with cheap, rot-gut whiskey, and Sam and Louis were readying the kitchen for the evening rush. A stagecoach was due at around five in the afternoon, bringing with it as many as twenty new customers, including its escort; usually a small detachment of cavalry or a dozen troopers, but it could be as many as sixteen, depending upon the number of passengers and the value of the cargo. They, along with up to six passengers, the driver, and his guard and, of course, the station guards, and one or two locals, would keep the dining room and saloon hopping well into the wee hours.

The guards, all armed with seven-shot Spencer rifles, were also about their duty, and they were wary and alert, being well aware of the more than a dozen Indian attacks along the Trail over the last several months.

A guard was stationed in each of the two twenty-five foot towers located at each end of the property. The two towers provided a wide view over the river to east and the mountains to the west; they could see along the Trail for almost a mile in both directions. The other two guards were together, patrolling the open spaces to the rear and front of the station. To the rear of the station was a wide-open space that stretched almost three hundred yards to a sheer cliff face that rose upward almost three hundred feet, an impregnable edifice and the station's main line of defense to the west.

For more than an hour, White Eagle and Yellow Crow had been watching the goings on at the station. They were lying face down on top of a low bluff. White Eagle was propped up on his elbows, a pair of battered brass binoculars at his eyes. From his vantage point, he could see the activity, or lack of it, at the station. He could also watch the progress of his warriors, led by Broken Nose, as they crept slowly through the shallow waters of the Purgatoire, hidden from view by the high riverbank.

For almost a half an hour, Broken Nose and his warriors crept along the river bank until at last he was opposite the northernmost watch tower and could see the guard sitting staring out along the trail. From where he was to the top of the tower was approximately 180 yards; it was close to the extreme distance for a bow shot, and one only an expert could even think of making, and Broken Nose was certainly that, an expert. He turned to face the bluff where he knew White Eagle was watching and raised his hand to let him know that he was in position.

On the bluff, White Eagle saw the signal, looked at Yellow Crow, nodded, and raised his arm to signal Broken Nose.

Broken Nose smiled, took an arrow from the quiver at his back, raised his head, checked for the wind – the air was still, not even a hint of a breeze stirred the leaves of the trees overhead – and he put the arrow to the bowstring.

The bow, unlike those used on horseback, was heavy, and designed for use on foot. Broken Nose took several deep breaths, slowly raised the bow, pulling back the string as he did so, until it was at full draw; the ninety pounds it took to pull required little effort by the muscular Comanche. For a second he held it, then... whoosh. It was gone, winging its way in a great arch, over the Trail, and down again to find its mark. Thuck. It slammed into the side of the guard's neck, the steel point splintering the vertebrate and cutting the spinal cord as it tore through and out the other side. The guard, paralyzed, pitched over sideways against the tower's rail. The rail cracked, gave way, and he plunged silently to the dirt floor below. The only sound was that of his lifeless body hitting the ground.

To the south, Yellow Crow had made a similar shot, with equal success. The way was now clear for White Eagle and the rest of his warriors to cross the trail to the front of the station. The two guards to the rear of the building were quickly dispatched. Two swift and deadly slashes left them lying silently on the dirt, the life blood pumping from their necks.

Seconds later, White Eagle and his men were inside the store, dining room, and kitchen.

Inside, Will Robbin was in the process of cleaning one of the display rifles. He was taken completely by surprise. The heavy Minnie ball from the chief's Sharps slammed into his chest, hurling him backward into the display cabinets. The glass shattered under the impact, and he was showered with razor-sharp shards and spears of glass, but he didn't care, he was already dying.

In the kitchen, Sam and Louis heard the shot and the breaking glass and looked wildly around for weapons. The only thing ready to hand was a large meat cleaver. Sam grabbed it and ran to the open doorway, only to be met by a wildly screaming warrior who rammed his lance into his gut. Sam dropped the cleaver, grabbed the lance with both hands, staggered backward, dragging the Indian with him, and collapsed. Louis was already gone, having leaped through the window and out onto the hard-packed dirt, running as hard as he could. He'd not gone more than twenty yards when he was hit in the back by two arrows. The impacts pitched him forward and for several yards his legs carried him on, his gait now a stagger, only his forward speed holding him upright, until, finally, he pitched forward onto his face and lay still.

In the saloon, Jed, too, heard the shot, as did the two drifters. Jed grabbed his shotgun from below the counter and raised it. One of the drifters drew his pistol; the other drifter was unarmed and ran for the back door.

The batwing doors at the front flew open and in charged a half-dozen Comanche. Jed, panicked, raised the shotgun and, without thinking, pulled both triggers. The leading warrior was hurled backward by the impact of both loads. Two more went down under the rapid fire from the drifter's Colt. The drifter at the back door barely had it open when he was hit between the shoulder blades by a flying tomahawk. The force of the impact threw him forward, through the door. He staggered out onto the dirt, fell to his knees, and was immediately grabbed by the hair. With a swift slash to his neck, the Comanche ended his life. With another, he lifted his scalp.

Inside the saloon, Jed and the drifter had no time to reload their weapons; they quickly succumbed to the knives and tomahawks of more than a dozen warriors. In only seconds they lay dead, their faces, throats, arms, and chests a mass of cuts, stabs and slashes. They lay together on the boards in a single, vast pool of blood.

And then it was over. The attack had lasted no more than five minutes. Fourteen men lay dead, three of them Comanche. The bodies of the six white men were dragged from the building. The bodies of the four guards were left to lie where they fell. The three dead Comanche were placed, and secured, over the backs of their ponies.

White Eagle walked slowly around the store, making a mental note of the stock. He wasn't interested in food, trinkets, or tools. He wanted guns and ammunition.

The haul was seven Spencer repeating rifles, six Sharps rifles, and twelve assorted pistols, along with a half dozen cases of ammunition and more than a dozen Bowie knives of various sizes. He had hoped for more, but was happy enough. He now had firearms enough for almost half of his warriors.

Less than thirty minutes after the attack, they were gone, disappeared back into the mountains. Robbin's

Hole was no more. By five o'clock, when the Overland Mail stagecoach and its military escort arrived, the building was no more than a pile of glowing embers. The bloody bodies of its one-time inhabitants lay around it. The arrows and missing scalps an unmistakable message: White Eagle was taking his revenge.

Chapter 17

O'Sullivan rose early, well before sunup, on Sunday morning. He hadn't slept well. The preparations of the past several days were complete; the command was ready to leave, only the doing of it was left.

When reveille had sounded at six o'clock, he was already washed, shaved and dressed and on his second cup of coffee. He had arranged the night before to meet with his officers and senior NCOs for breakfast. This he did, and, after more assurances and last minute checks that all was in order, they walked the few yards from the dining room to the parade ground. Their horses, the men, pack animals and artillery were waiting. Knowing where they were going, O'Sullivan had ordered the wagons left behind; their contents were loaded onto the mules. Water would be scarce, and so it would have be taken with them. Ten mules each carried four wooden casks filled with the precious liquid.

For much of their journey into the mountains, the two heavy guns would have to carried, Major Anthony had supplied O'Sullivan with six of the largest mules he had ever seen, even during his jaunt into northern Alabama with the erstwhile Colonel Streight. They were bigger even than many of the cavalry horses, and they looked mean. For the first part of trip, fifteen or so miles, they would not carry a load, to keep them fresh and

151

strong for the ordeal they would be required to endure once the gun carriages had to be dismantled.

By nine o'clock that morning, they were ready to leave. O'Sullivan, with Coffin close behind, raised his arm, and shouted the order, "Forwaaard Ho!"

The officers were at the heads of their respective companies, Daly leading. In column of threes, at the walk, the command left Fort Lyon, and headed southwest on the Santa Fe Trail toward Newsom's Station.

It was already afternoon when they arrived at the mouth of the dry riverbed, a vast open area, mostly flat, but strewn with rocks and boulders of every shape and size. Deep trenches, some eight or more feet deep, spread like gigantic, spidery fingers from the riverbed to the Trail. The sheer escarpments that rose upward almost vertically on both sides of the riverbed reflected the heat of the afternoon sun directly downward onto its stone surface. It was a wild, desolate, and unforgiving place, a portent of what was yet to come, and none of it good.

It took no more than a cursory inspection by O'Sullivan and his officers to determine that from here on the going would be difficult. The guns would have to be disassembled and loaded onto the pack animals, a process that would take at least an hour.

"If we make more'n ten miles a day over that," O'Sullivan said, staring up the arroyo, "I shall be very surprised, so I will. It's getting late. By the time the guns are loaded it will be too late to make much of a start.

152

We'll camp here for the night. There's no tellin' when we'll find another place big enough for us all. It'll be rough, even here, but it can't be helped. We'll make an early start in the morning. In the meantime, unload the animals, get 'em fed and settled.

"Lieutenant Warwick, Whitworth, have my tent pitched over there, up against the cliff face, then have the men build fires. There's plenty of dead wood lyin' around.

"Bear Claw." He turned to face the Shoshone scout. "Walk with me; you too, Sergeant Major. The rest of you stay here. I want to go see what we're up against."

The three men set off, on foot toward the mouth of the arroyo. The officers, with the exception of Carson and Keogh who stood and stared after them, went about their tasks.

"Hope he breaks his goddamn neck," Keogh snarled.

"We couldn't get that lucky," Carson said, still staring after the three diminishing figures, "but who knows?"

For almost an hour the three men walked, sometimes stumbling, sometimes stopping to sit, rest, and drink water from their canteens. The ground over which they traveled was rough and undulating, blanketed with sand, loose rocks, pebbles, and sharp shards of stone. The trail, if it could be called that, was bordered by enormous piles of rock, giant boulders that had split away from the cliff face. While the riverbed was fairly wide, it was little short of a nightmare to negotiate. The

153

heat of the day was oppressive. The glare of the sun, reflected from the cliff face, burned their skin. The air was still, not a hint of a breeze. Farther along the arroyo, not even a hundred yards from where they were sitting, they could see the haze shimmering above the rocks. It was a stark, unforgiving world, but somehow very beautiful.

The sweat of their bodies soaked into the rough woolen cloth of their uniforms. That, combined with the fine sand that worked its way into every nook and cranny, every fold in the cloth, turned their clothing into a damp abrasive that rubbed the skin raw.

"Holy Mother Mary," O'Sullivan said, breathless, as he sat down on a large rock. "There's no way we can make any sort of time at all over this." He looked upward, scouring the ridges more than a thousand feet above. "This is a bloody death trap, so it is. All anyone would need do is sit up there and hurl rocks down on us; we wouldn't stand a chance." He shook his head, looked first at Coffin, who could only nod his agreement, then at Bear Claw.

The Shoshone simply shrugged his shoulders; he seemed little troubled by the rough going, or by the heat.

"Is there any sign that they came this way, Bear Claw?"

The scout nodded. "Much horses, some with steel feet, some not. See dung... some old, some new... three, maybe four days, many ponies come this way."

"White Eagle?"

The scout smiled, two of his front teeth were missing. "Not know, Colonel. Bear Claw not able to see into past, just dung.

O'Sullivan smiled at the scout's attempt at humor. Funny it might have been; helpful it was not.

O'Sullivan stood, stretched, gathered up his canteen from the top of the rock where he'd been sitting, looked on up the trail and shook his head. "No point goin' farther, it's just more of the same. How long before the going gets any easier?" he asked the scout.

"One day; no more. The way will become easy, then we go up mountain, maybe another day, maybe two. One more day to forks, then only wilderness."

"Only wilderness?" O'Sullivan stared at him, dumbfounded. "What the hell is this, then?"

Bear Claw smiled, but did not reply. He just stared back stoically back at O'Sullivan.

"Better start back, then. Nothing to be gained out here. At least we know now what to expect." He turned, shouldered his canteen, pulled the brim of his hat down to shade his eyes, and started back the way they had come. An hour later, they were back with the command. The camp had been raised, the fires set, and the air was filled with a mouthwatering aroma of roasting beef, compliments of Major Anthony and Fort Lyon.

Most of the men bedded down early that evening, including O'Sullivan and most of the officers. Only Carson and Keogh stayed by one of the fires, talking quietly together, long into the night.

By nine o'clock the following morning, the animals had been loaded, the fires put out, and they were back in the saddle, now in single file, heading westward along the arroyo.

The going, as O'Sullivan had predicted, was slow. The cavalry horses had little trouble picking their way along the rock-strewn riverbed. The pack animals, however, heavily loaded as they were, did not find the going easy. They required frequent stops, to rest and drink. The water was carefully rationed, the animals being their first priority.

Every hour, the column stopped for ten minutes to rest; every other hour, the mules were unloaded and allowed to rest for forty-five minutes. During those rest periods, the horses were unsaddled and their backs were cleaned of the sand and dust that infiltrated the saddle blankets and rubbed their backs raw. And the sun continued to climb until by noon it was almost directly overhead, and the riverbed had heated up to almost unbearable temperatures.

By late afternoon, when O'Sullivan called the final halt for the day, they had traveled, by Coffin's estimation, no more than seven miles. They were all, men, horses and mules, exhausted.

But it was not yet over. The animals had to be tended to, fed, made comfortable, and settled down for the night. The men were so tired O'Sullivan ordered that tents need be pitched only if their owners wanted them.

If they did, they must pitch them for themselves. The order was given for the benefit of the officers and senior NCOs who would normally have them pitched for them. That night, he wanted to be sure that all who needed rest would get it. And not a single tent was raised. Campfires were kept to a minimum. The evening meal, such as it was, consisted of crackers and cheese; coffee was a must, and was served right up until the last man had wrapped himself in his blanket.

As darkness closed in over the arroyo, the command camped where it had stopped. The campfires stretched back along the draw for almost a mile. More than three hundred blue bundles lay scattered in odd, assorted groups along the riverbed. The campfires, strung out like a ribbon of glowing jewels in the night, cast flickering red waves of light over the rock walls, boulders, ridges, and bluffs, turning the landscape into an undulating, nightmarish world that played havoc with the imagination, enhanced by the by the cacophony of the night. The arroyo crackled, hummed, and echoed with the noises of the insects, wild animals and predator birds of the night.

High on a bluff, some quarter mile to the west, two of four Comanche warriors crept quietly away from the edge of the cliff from which they had been observing the blue coat soldiers. The other two remained where they were, watching....

Chapter 18

High Mountains of Colorado, August 22

The soldiers reached the forks of the riverbed at its highest point around two o'clock in the afternoon of the fourth day. The arroyo flattened and opened up into a wide-open space some quarter mile wide that stretched away toward the west, a high desert strewn with giant rocks and boulders that sloped downward slightly for almost a mile.

They were now some six thousand feet above sea level and the vast grasslands to the east. To the south, the mountains rose ever upward, the outline of James Peak just visible against the skyline. To the west and north, it was more of the same, although the skyline there was somewhat lower. As far as the eye could see, the ragged terrain stretched endlessly in every direction. It was a wild and desolate world of towering peaks, bluffs, ridges, crags, rifts and deep defiles, stark and forbidding.

Several hundred yards on, they could see what appeared to a branch of dry river bed. It forked off the left, to the south; just beyond it was another that also headed toward the south but at a slightly different angle. Beyond that one, a third forked away to right, the north.

O'Sullivan called a halt, ordered the saddles removed from the horses, with the exception of those of the officers, several of the senior NCO, including Coffin, and the scouts. He also ordered the packs and guns be unloaded from the mules. They had, he decided, come far enough for today; now was the time to scout ahead.

"Bear Claw, Lieutenant Warwick, Sergeant Major Coffin, you're with me. We'll go on ahead. Lieutenant Daly, you take Lieutenant Whitworth an' Nitis," O'Sullivan said, nodding toward one of the Apache scouts, "an' go take a look along that first fork to the left. Captain Carson, Lieutenant Keogh, you take Dahkeya–"

"If you don't mind, Colonel," Carson said, quietly, "we'll leave the Apache with you."

"Very well." O'Sullivan saw no point in arguing. "Go scout the second fork. Dahkeya, you stay with Bear Claw. Go to it. Be back before dark, all of you.

They set off along the now flat, wide riverbed together; Daly peeled away to the left, Carson a few minutes later. O'Sullivan and his small group walked their horses onward toward the fork that branched away to the right.

The branch was quite wide, much wider than O'Sullivan was expecting, and it looked as if the going was easier, too, due to the level riverbed, he supposed.

He called a halt and the five men dismounted. Bear Claw and Dahkeya walked slowly along the draw, one on either side. O'Sullivan, Warwick and Coffin stood together and watched as they inched their way forward.

"This isn't it," O'Sullivan muttered to himself.

"Did you say something, Colonel?" Warwick asked.

"I said, this isn't it. Just a feelin', but I don't think so."

The feeling was confirmed some fifteen minutes later when the two scouts rejoined them. Bear Claw was shaking his head.

"Some, maybe, but no war party. Few signs. Maybe that way." He pointed westward along the main branch of the dry riverbed. "There are more forks, six, maybe seven more. We go see, yes?"

O'Sullivan nodded and the five men remounted and continued the walk westward. One by one, they discounted three more branches until at the forth one that veered away to the right, Bear Claw nodded. "Two, maybe three days. Many ponies pass this way, but they come from the south, then turn west, that way." Again, he pointed along the now wide flat plain that stretched away in front of them.

"They didn't take the fork? How many?" O'Sullivan asked.

"One hundred... more... one hundred twenty." Bear Claw looked at Dahkeya, questioningly; the Apache nodded.

"We go see, yes?" Bear Claw asked, waving his arm to indicate the direction.

"We go see," O'Sullivan agreed.

They found it just before sundown.

The trail split into two; one continued westward, the other veered sharply to the north.

"Which way, Bear Claw? When?

"Both way. Main war party go there." Bear Claw pointed to the trail west. "Many ponies go that way. Maybe two days, no more. Some take other trail. Twenty-five, thirty ponies. We go that way, yes?" Again, he pointed along the trail that led to the west.

"Yeah." O'Sullivan nodded. "But not today. Why'd they split up, I wonder?" There was no answer from either of the scouts, or Warwick.

"Maybe they know we're after 'em," Coffin said.

"I'd bet on it," O'Sullivan agreed, "but there's nothing we can do about that. If that village is up here somewhere, they'd be watchin' the trails: these trails." He looked uneasily around. "White Eagle ain't nobody's fool, that's certain. I'd bet me last dollar he knows we're here, an' that ain't good. Let's get back to the others. It'll soon be dark, an' I don't want to get caught out here on our own. Never know what might be waitin' for us down the trail, an' I ain't talking about animals. Leastwise, not the four-legged ones."

Meanwhile Daly, Whitworth and Nitis had gone as far as they could go along their fork in the river and had turned back and were now following along after O'Sullivan and his group.

Carson and Keogh, however, were by now more than two miles to the south and still following the trail. It wasn't that they had any real idea that they might find anything, more it was an intense desire to get away from

161

O'Sullivan, at least for a while, and so they meandered onward. By five o'clock, with the sun already just above the mountaintops to the west, they were some three miles from the main body of the command and perhaps as many as five miles from where O'Sullivan had found what he had been looking for.

"Best we think about headin' back," Keogh said.

"What the hell for?"

"'Cause the colonel said we should be back by dark, is why."

"He can go to hell, and he ain't no goddamn colonel."

"Yeah, but...."

"Yeah, but my ass. We'll keep going, at least for a while. Give the son-of-a-bitch something to think about."

Keogh heard something up ahead. "Shusssh," he said, quietly. "What the hell was that?"

They sat and listened, then Carson heard it, the sound of hooves on rock.

"Quick, grab your rifle," Carson whispered. "Get down. Hide the horses. Something's coming this way."

The two men dismounted, hid the horses behind a pile of rocks, then scrambled up onto a low bluff that provided them with a view, though somewhat restricted, of the arroyo ahead. They were just in time. Two hundred yards away, five Comanche warriors mounted on ponies were making their way slowly toward them.

Keogh grinned as he whispered to Carson, "Easy pickins, Captain." He cranked the lever of his Spencer. The noise echoed along the draw like a pistol shot. The five warriors were immediately on the alert and reaching for their weapons.

"Goddamn it, Keogh," Carson yelled, cranking his own Spencer and bringing it to his shoulder. "Why the hell didn't you wait for my word?"

Bam! The rifle punched back into his shoulder.

Bam! Keogh fired less than a second later.

Two of the Indians pitched backward and fell to the ground. The others, their ponies spinning in panic, made a valiant effort to bring their own weapons to bear, but before they could, the two soldiers had fired again and two more of them fell twisting and turning to land on their backs on the rock floor. The fifth warrior, turned, kicked his pony and sped off along the arroyo in the direction from which he had come. Two more shots rang out. One of them clipped the fleeing warrior's upper arm, the other missed, and he flew onward, whipping his pony to greater and greater efforts. Then he was gone, leaving Carson and Keogh standing, staring after him.

The wounded warrior did not slow his pace until he was sure that he was out of range of the blue coat rifles, and that he was not being followed. Then he traveled quickly through the mountains, making a wide circle from the south to the west. Finally he headed northeast toward White Eagle's village on the banks of the Smoky

Hill Fork River, stopping only to rest and water the pony.

Carson was as mad as hell. "Goddamn it, Keogh. You stupid son-of-a-bitch. We let him get away. If we'd waited just a moment more, we'd a had 'em all. You silly bastard. I oughta shoot your goddamn ass; that's what I oughta do."

Keogh was unperturbed by his outburst. "Hell, Cap," he said, grinning broadly. "We got four of 'em. Let's get us some hair."

Almost five miles away to the north, O'Sullivan and his group, now reunited with Daly's small contingent, heard the six shots echoing through the mountains.

"What the hell was that?" Coffin asked.

O'Sullivan shook his head, "Dunno. Maybe Carson found somethin'. We need to find out. Let's go."

O'Sullivan's group reached the main body of the command just as night fell. They entered camp by the light of thirty or more fires. The air was filled with the aroma of cooking: ham, beans, coffee. They arrived only minutes before Carson and Keogh, who joined them at the fireside, plates and mugs in hand.

"So," O'Sullivan said, as they sat, "what was the shootin' all about?"

Carson looked at him across the crackling fire. The flames turned his face dark red and accentuated its lines, elongating it, and exaggerating the Van Dyke beard to a point where he might easily have been mistaken for the Devil himself. Only the horns were missing. "You heard it then?"

"I did. What was it all about?"

"Nothing. Nothing at all. Just a bobcat among the rocks. We didn't get him."

O'Sullivan stared at him and shook his head. "There's be no more of that. If they don't already know we're here, which I'm sure they do, indiscriminate firing will bring 'em down on us in a hurry, so it will."

"Hah," Keogh said, with his mouth full. He swallowed. "So what? There's more'n 'nough of us here to see off a bunch o' goddamn savages, no matter how many of 'em there might be."

O'Sullivan simply shook his head, swilled down the last of his coffee, rose to his feet, and headed for his tent, too irritated for words.

Chapter 19

White Eagle's Village, August 23

White Eagle's village was set among the high mountains of the eastern Colorado Territory, approximately forty miles to the north of James Peak, sixty miles west of Newsom's Station, and perhaps seventy-five miles west of Fort Lyon. It was situated in a small, isolated valley on the banks of the Smoky Hill Fork River. The valley, more river basin, was less than a half-mile in diameter through which the river meandered until it widened into an almost circular lake some five hundred yards across. The lake was surrounded by a broad band of green and fertile land upon which White Eagle's band of Kwahadi Comanche had built their village. As many as a hundred teepees lined the north shore of the lake. It was home to almost 350 warriors, women and children.

All around the lake, only a few hundred yards from its shores, just beyond the point where the fertile strip turned from green to desert, the mountains rose upward more than three thousand feet, a vast wilderness of peaks, ridges, scarps, bluffs, arroyos, gorges and sheer cliffs. Entry into the valley was achieved by one of three routes: the river gorge to the east, the same to the west, and by a narrow, arroyo that cut through the mountains on the north side of the lake. The arroyo was easy to negotiate, but not easy to find, a cleft in the escarpment. From a distance, it appeared to be nothing more than a dip in the skyline beyond the stands of massive, old growth pines that lay across the terrain before it.

It was an idyllic spot, the little valley, protected from the winds that often howled through the mountains in winter, and, because of its elevation, cool in summer. The lake teemed with bass, easily visible in its deep crystal waters.

Smoke spiraled upward from a dozen campfires, the voices of children laughing echoed faintly over the lake, and the two women sat, side-by-side, on a log at the water's edge.

It had been more than a month since Elva had been abducted from Newsom's station. She hadn't been close to the man, but he had given her a home, clothing, and a little money, for which she had been grateful, but all that was now gone, and the future... it held... as far as she could tell, nothing. She had no idea where she was, of how far from civilization she might be. But life in the village had, up until now, been good. She had been treated well, by White Eagle, the women of the village, and even by the fierce Yellow Crow. The children of the village, though they were in awe of her color, loved to be with her.

And then there was White Eagle himself. He expected her to prepare his meals, wash and mend his clothes, and.... The night, almost three weeks ago, he had taken her to his bed, she had been petrified with fear, but it had been a pleasant experience, one she soon began to look forward to, although the man had little to say to her, ever.

Now there was Dora and her children. At first, Yellow Crow had insisted that she was to be his woman, but for some reason he kept to himself, White Eagle would not allow it. Yellow Crow was, at first, angry, but once the boundaries had been laid, he didn't argue. White Eagle was chief in all things and was to be obeyed without question; this Elva had understood that first night when Yellow Crow had pulled her down from his horse. She also understood, though only lately, that Yellow Crow loved his chief, and, even more so, respected him, both as a leader and as a warrior.

167

The two women had been sitting together beside the lake for more than an hour that morning, speaking softly to each other, watching the children playing. Dora's two girls had, as most children do, quickly made friends with those of the village. Language, though none of them understood each other, was never a problem.

Elva looked up, along the river toward the west. She didn't know why, perhaps it was just a feeling. She didn't know the time, but she knew it must be around mid-morning by the position of the sun. She was about to look away when she saw them: the warriors were returning.

As she watched, two warriors leapt onto the backs of their ponies and galloped the more than quarter mile to join the returning warriors, and they were in a hurry. The two had returned to the village late the previous afternoon and, finding White Eagle gone, and not knowing where, they had had no option but to wait for him.

Now, as she watched, they talked agitatedly to the chief, their arms waving, pointing into the mountains to the south. Even at that distance, she could see the stern look on his face. The war party entered the village a few minutes later. The three dead warriors were gently taken from the backs of their ponies and laid in one of the teepees. Later that evening, they would be sent to the home of the Great Spirit.

"You." He pointed at Elva. "Come." He walked the short distance to his teepee, lifted the flap, and walked inside. She followed a moment later.

"We go. You make ready. Tell her." He waved his hand in the general direction of the nearby teepee where Dora and the children were now living.

She looked at him, a little bewildered. "Go? Where? Why?"

"Many blue coat soldiers come. Not safe here. We go."

"Soldiers?" she asked, her heart beating faster. "When?"

"Hah," he said, with a tight smile. "You not worry. They not find you. I keep you safe." And with that, he left the teepee, leaving Elva wide-eyed and wondering.

By nightfall, the preparations for the move had been completed. They would leave for the high mountains before dawn the following morning.

Chapter 20

The High Mountains, August 23

The command broke camp at daybreak. As the sun rose over the Great Plains to the east, they set out in column of two toward the fork in the arroyo where the war party had split into two.

Again, the going was slow. Even though the riverbed was now much wider and flatter, it was still necessary for the guns to be carried by the mules. Even so, by ten o'clock they had reached their objective and O'Sullivan had called a halt. The animals were unloaded and rested for an hour. O'Sullivan called the officers and senior NCOs together.

"This is where Bear Claw and Dahkeya say that White Eagle split his force less than two days ago. Some went that way, twenty, maybe as many as thirty. The rest, the main party, continued on along the wadi, that way.

"Captain Carson. You an' Lieutenant Keogh; you'll take Company G an' follow the trail taken by the smaller force. You'll take with you rations for two days. If by that time you've found nothing, you'll return here and wait, either until I return with the rest of the command, or until I send for you. Company K will continue on after the main party. Captain Morgan, you're also with me.

"Now, Captain Carson, hear this. Our task is to find White Eagle and persuade him to come in, 'an that's what I intend to do. That bein' so, should you find them, you are not, I repeat, not under any circumstances, to engage them. You stay well back, follow, watch 'em, and send a rider to report to me. Understood?"

"Of course, Colonel. I am to stay well back, follow them, watch them, and send a rider to report to you. I am not to engage the enemy." It was said with a smile, but there was an underlying edge to both his voice and his stare.

"Very well, mount up. Let's get after 'em."

Carson, Keogh and Company G, some ninety-three troopers, plus officers and NCOs, made their way slowly along the draw, following what obviously was a well-worn trail. The going was easy and there was room enough for them to proceed in column of twos. For several hours, the column headed in a generally northern direction, swinging eastward for a distance, then back to the northwest.

They'd traveled some nine or ten miles through rifts and valleys when Carson finally decided it was time to call a halt for the night. He felt good about the spot he'd chosen. It was located at a widening of the riverbed, a place far enough from the high cliffs and sheer rock faces that surrounded them for him to be reasonably sure that he was safe from ambush from above. He posted pickets to the north and south, ordered the horses be fed and settled for the night, and then the evening meal be prepared. The meal would be no more than crackers, cheese and water to drink. Fires were not to be lit. Even smoking was to be kept to a minimum, and hidden from any possible prying eyes. Tents had been left with the main body of the command, and so, by ten o'clock, they were all, with the exception of the two officers and the pickets, wrapped in their blankets either asleep or listening to the sounds of night desert.

High on a bluff, a quarter mile away to the west, White Eagle, Yellow Crow, and of his six warriors had been following and watching Carson's column for several hours, since before dark.

Far away to the southwest, O'Sullivan had also bedded his command down for the night and, though he didn't know it for sure, he had an all-powerful feeling, an itching of the skin, that he, too, was being watched.

Broken Nose and three warriors kept themselves well-hidden as they continued their vigil through the night.

The following morning, Carson and Keogh rose early. Neither of them had managed to get much sleep; the blankets did little to relieve the painful effects of rocky, unforgiving ground upon which they lay, but it was more than that. They had been restless to begin with and had sat together, talking long into the night, ever watchful, listening to the changing of the pickets at midnight, and again a four o'clock in the morning. Both were glad to see the first streaks of daylight in the eastern sky. They were ready to be back on the trail they were both sure held nothing but danger.

By eight o'clock, the column was mounted and proceeding north; by nine o'clock, they found themselves at the mouth of a narrow canyon, no more than a hundred yards wide. Carson raised his right arm, a silent signal for the column to a halt.

The wadi meandered onward, threading its way between sheer rock walls that towered upward several hundred feet. The air in the canyon was still, not even a hint of a breeze, and hot, oppressively so. Not a sound could be heard, other than the click of steel-shod hooves on the rocky floor that echoed around the canyon walls, or the occasional snort of horse in need of water, or the sneeze of a trooper with dust in his nose. The atmosphere was claustrophobic, and Carson's skin crawled. *If ever there were a place for an ambush, this would be it.*

For several moments, he sat still in the saddle, his hands folded together on the pommel of his saddle. *I don't like it. Not one goddamn bit.*

"Walk the column forward, Lieutenant Keogh. Have the men draw their carbines and chamber a round, and tell 'em to keep a sharp lookout, *and do it quietly.*"

Keogh nodded, turned his horse, and proceeded back along the column, whispering the order over and over. As he did so, like a wave proceeding along the column, each man drew his Spencer from its scabbard and worked the action, loading a cartridge into the breach and cocking the action. Quiet, it was not. The clatter as they loaded their weapons echoed off the canyon wall made Carson cringe as he listened for the slightest sound that would indicate an imminent danger. Nothing.

More than a quarter mile to the north, behind a ridge at the far end of the canyon, White Eagle watched through the battered glasses, and smiled. The blue coats were nervous. *Good.*

Carson scoured the canyon floor and the tops of the canyon walls. Nothing. For several minutes, he stayed where he was, sweeping the glasses back and forth. Still nothing.

He shivered, not from cold, but from one of those, *someone just walked over my grave* kind of feelings. Then he shrugged, looked at Keogh, shrugged again, replaced his glasses in the pouch on his saddle, drew his Henry rifle, checked the load, worked the action, raised his hand and signaled the column forward.

White Eagle watched as the blue coats slowly entered the canyon, and again he smiled.

More than twenty miles away to southwest, O'Sullivan was following the ever-widening dry riverbed as it meandered westward, then to the north, curving through the mountains toward... more mountains.

The terrain was stark, desolate, and he was beginning to worry about water. They had started out with plenty, but after almost five days with no signs of replenishment, he was more than a little concerned. There was perhaps enough in the casks for one more day, but they were now well beyond the point of no return. They did not have enough, he was sure, to keep the animals alive long enough to make it back to Newsom's station. They had to find water, and they had to find it soon.

He consulted Bear Claw and the two Apache scouts, but they were now well beyond the point where the scouts had any knowledge of what might lie ahead. He had no option but to continue onward and hope.

A little after eleven o'clock that morning, Carson and his column had emerged from the north end of the column without incident, much to his and Keogh's relief. They were proceeding now at a leisurely pace; the direction of the wadi was slowly turning toward the west.

Chapter 21

White Eagle's Village, August 24

Elva, Dora, the children, and the rest of the Comanche families left the village early the following morning. Everything that could be moved, all of their personal belongings, clothing, pots, pans, bedding, had been loaded onto travois and transported northward through the hidden arroyo. Only the teepees remained standing by the shores of the pristine lake. The fires of the night burned low, no more than embers. Wisps of smoke from the dampened cook fires inside the teepees rose from openings at the tops of the lodge poles.

White Eagle, Yellow Crow, Broken Nose, all of the warriors, were gone. Elva had not set eyes on the chief since he had given instructions for them to make ready to leave. With the exception of a few elderly members of the band, perhaps a dozen or so, that had insisted on remaining, the village was deserted.

It was just before one o'clock in the afternoon when Carson and his troop emerged from the arroyo onto a wide bluff almost a thousand feet above the Smoky Hill Fork River at the east end of the river valley. The lake and its basin lay spread out before them. The view over White Eagle's village, more than a mile way to the northwest, was stunning.

Carson looked at Keogh and grinned. Together, they reached for their glasses. All was quiet.

"It looks deserted," Keogh said.

"No, I can see people among the teepees. Not many, but they're there. See?" Carson pointed. "There, to the right. Two, no three, sitting. And over there," again he pointed, "two more, and over there... I make it close to twenty. Looks like old men and women. He must be gone, hunting, killing white folk, I shouldn't wonder."

Keogh nodded. "So what we gonna do? Send word to the colonel?"

"Hell, no."

"But he gave strict orders—"

"Yeah, so he did, and so did General Sherman, and I'll take Sherman's orders over that son-of-a-bitch's every time. Let's go get 'em."

To enter the valley, they first had to turn east along the top of the bluff. The way down to the river valley was a winding trail of more than a mile that eventually gave way to the broad, green fertile strip of land that bordered the Smoky Hill Fork. From there, they had to cross the shallow river and then ride west along riverbank for another mile until, eventually, they saw the first grouping of teepees not more than two hundred yards away in front of them.

A little more than an hour later, Carson held up his hand, halted the column, and listened. All seemed quiet. Here and there, a wisp of smoke rose lazily upward from the tops of the loge poles.

He pulled his Henry rifle from its scabbard, worked the action, and turned in the saddle to look back along the column. Every man held either a pistol or a rifle.

He raised his hand in the air. Keogh, his mouth set in tight-lipped smile, nodded, thumbed back the hammer on his Colt Army revolver, and waited for Carson's signal.

Carson swept his hand down and dug his spurs into his horse's flank. The horse reared, snorted, and then set off along the riverbank at full gallop. The rest of the column followed close behind, whooping and shouting, the Company G colors and guidon fluttering.

In the village, the old men – not old men at all, but warriors – leaped to their feet and took cover behind a series of rocks a tree trunks that White Eagle had had placed at strategic points throughout the settlement as part of his preparations the previous evening. The trap had been set, and tripped, and Carson and his company were riding full tilt into it.

As Carson and the leading elements of Company G entered the village, the now hidden warriors waited, watched by the lone figure high on the bluff. White Eagle, a terrifying spectacle in full war paint and headdress, stood with his hand in the air, holding his rifle high above his head. He waited until Carson's leading elements had reached the center of the village, and then he dropped his hand, and they opened fire. From within the village, and from the bluffs and ridges that ringed it, some fifty rifles sent a hail of Minnie balls into the speeding troopers. These were followed by as many, and more, arrows.

Three men went down immediately, followed by two more, and then another. Six more troopers were wounded, but managed to stay in the saddle.

Carson, taken by surprise, was quick to assess the situation. Without slowing, he yelled, "IT'S A TRAP. KEEP GOING. HEAD FOR THE PASS ON THE OTHER SIDE." He put his head down, leaned forward along the neck of his horse, and slammed his spurs into its flanks. The horse lengthened its stride and seemed to leap forward, flying through the village as if it had wings. Keogh was only feet behind him, and the rest of the column streamed out behind them, kicking and whipping their mounts, urging them onward.

Two more men reared up in the saddle under the impact of the heavy caliber Minnie balls. Another pitched over backward and to the ground, rolling in the dirt. The shaft of the arrow that had pierced the side of head, killing him almost instantly, snapped, leaving several inches of bloody shaft protruding from his skull.

On the high bluffs to the south, White Eagle watched, and smiled as he saw Carson's men begin to slow, and panic, not knowing which way to turn. His warriors continued to pour fire, Minnie balls and arrows down upon them with devastating effect.

But Carson was not yet done. He looked back and saw his men begin to falter, and he wheeled his horse and sped back toward them with Keogh following close behind. He yelled at the top of his voice, firing his Colt first in this direction and then that, and hitting nothing. And then, with Carson yelling and screaming at them, the Company rallied, and they were off again, heading for the pass at the west end of the valley at full gallop.

Keogh hauled back on the reins, jerking the horse's head to the side. It staggered sideways, stumbled, dropped to one knee, almost throwing him. Then it gathered itself, leapt up, reared and charged after Carson. The horse had not taken more than a half-dozen strides when an arrow slammed into Keogh. It hit high on the right side of his chest, just below the shoulder. The impact threw him sideways and backward, out of the saddle, and down to land on his shoulders, under the hooves of the galloping horses. Hundreds of them, so it seemed, hammered the ground around him. Only one hit him, clipping his right calf and sending spears of pain up his leg. For a moment, he lay half-stunned, then he tried to sit up. He raised his head, stared after the cloud of dust that was now all that was left of Company G, as it careened on along the riverbank and away through the pass and into the mountains beyond.

As soon as he thought he was out of range, Carson hauled his horse to a stop, reached for his glasses, and surveyed the scene he had just left. From one end of the village to the other, horses were down, some lay still, some were squirming and trying to rise. From one end to the other, the soldiers of his company lay in the dirt, most of them dead, hit multiple times by Minnie balls and arrows. Some, a few, maybe five that he could see, were still alive, among them, Lieutenant Ewan Keogh. And he watched as two of White Eagle's warriors ran from cover, grabbed Keogh by the arms, and dragged him away, out of sight. Carson shuddered, then turned, put spurs to horse, and galloped westward, following what remained of his company along the riverbank and into the mountains.

The attack had lasted all of six minutes, no more than the amount of time it had taken for Company G to gallop the length of the village from east to west. It had been costly. Thirty-two of Carson's men lay dead among the teepees. A dozen more were wounded, six of them still lay in the village. Three of those were already dying, the other three, including Keogh, were already captives, their fates... *Who the hell knows?*

He caught up with his men, and they rode on for perhaps another mile and then turned south into an arroyo that seemed to lead in the general direction he needed to go. He needed to find O'Sullivan and the rest of the command. But first....

He slowed his horse to a walk. There was a pain in his left upper arm. He rubbed it with his right hand, and gasped as the pain seared his upper arm. The cloth of his uniform was sticky. He looked sideways and found it soaked with blood. Just below the crown of his shoulder, there were two small holes in the sleeve. He undid the buttons down the front of jacket, shrugged his left shoulder, winced as the pain coursed through his arm, and with his right hand gently eased the coat down past his elbow. He probed the holes in his shirt gently with his fingers. To his relief, there was no hole in his shoulder, just a deep cut in the fatty part of his upper arm. He slipped his arm out of the jacket and circled it over his head. *No muscle damage, I think.* He shook his head, *Lucky, I guess, or maybe not. We'll see. That goddamn Irishman is going to love this.*

He slipped his arm back into the jacket and pulled it up back over his shoulder, buttoned it, kicked his horse to a fast walk, and resumed his search for the rest of the command

Carson had no illusions. He had disobeyed a direct and specific order, and the result had been a disaster. He was in serious trouble.

For maybe another mile, Company G followed the draw upward and southward until they reached the top of a ridge that offered a panoramic view of the valley they had recently left.

He called a halt and looked down upon the village in the distance to the east. He reached for his glasses, winced from the pain, changed hands and put the glasses to his eyes. The area was swarming with Indians, but even as far away as they were, he could see the blue of the bodies scattered along the riverbank.

The column moved onward and upward, heading south. They had not gone more than another mile when they were met by Sergeant Major Coffin along with two troopers and the scout Bear Claw.

182

White Eagle watched as the tail end of the column that was Company G disappeared into the distance. He would not pursue them. He well knew that as long as he had the advantage of the high ground, he could win. To follow the blue coats would be to give up that advantage, but it was more than that. There was work to do in the village.

Like ants, his warriors streamed down from the mountains and into the village where they were joined by those who had remained in ambush, and they went to work. The horses left behind by Company G were rounded up. The wounded prisoners were bound with their hands in front of them, set on horseback, and were led from the village, through the hidden gorge, and into the mountains. They tore down the teepees, turned the lodge poles into travois, and hauled them off into the mountains.

When all was done, White Eagle looked around the once pristine little river valley that had been his home. The riverbank was bare, the ground worn flat by the passage of thousands of footsteps over a period of a half-dozen years. Now only the bodies of the hated blue coats remained, and they would be left to rot where they, or until someone came for them. He knew they would, for he knew exactly where they were, and how many. Ho looked up at the distant peaks away to the south. He slowly nodded his head, his mouth set in a grim smile. It would not be long, and he would be ready for them.

Chapter 21

Abandoned Village, August 24, late afternoon

"Captain Carson." Coffin saluted. "What the hell happened? You've been wounded."

"Very observant, Sergeant Major." He didn't bother to return the salute. "Where is Colonel O'Sullivan?"

"Back that away, 'bout fifteen minutes or so. We heard the gunfire. What happened, sir?"

"None of your goddamn business. Now, show me the way, damn you."

Coffin did as he was told, turned his horse around, and headed back the way he had come. His three companions, and what was left of Company G, followed behind him. Not more than ten minutes later, they rounded a sharp bend in the wadi and were met by O'Sullivan and the rest of his command. He was a hundred yards, out front of the main column, accompanied by Captain Morgan and Lieutenants Daly and Warwick.

"What the hell happened, Captain? And where the hell is Lieutenant Keogh?" O'Sullivan shouted, angrily, although he already had a good idea.

Carson drew himself upright in the saddle, the reins in his right hand, his wounded left arm hanging limp by his side. "Sir, we found the Indian encampment early this afternoon. Apart from a few old men, it appeared to have been abandoned. I expected little or no resistance, so I ordered the Company to attack. I... was wrong, Colonel. It was an ambush.

"The oldsters were not what they appeared to be. They were, in fact, warriors. The second we entered the village, they took cover and opened fire. We also took a massive amount of fire from the surrounding hills. There had to have been at least two hundred of them hidden up there, waiting for us. Sir, they knew we were coming, and they were ready for us."

O'Sullivan stared at him, his face bright red with anger, his eyes narrow strips. The officers just to his rear stared stoically ahead. Coffin, just to Carson's right side, and out of sight of both Carson and O'Sullivan, sat astride his horse shaking his head in amazement.

"I gave you a direct order, Captain Carson, did I not? I ordered that under no circumstances were you to engage the enemy, did I not say exactly that?"

"You did, Colonel, but–"

"BUT?" O'Sullivan shouted, interrupting him. It was loud enough that even the men in the waiting column a hundred yards to the rear could hear it. "What the hell did you not understand? And I ask again, *Where in God's name is Lieutenant Keogh?*"

Carson took a deep breath, stared O'Sullivan in the eye and said, quietly, "Lieutenant Keogh is taken, Colonel."

"Taken? You mean he's dead, right?"

Carson shook his head. "Not dead, sir, wounded, a prisoner, and two more along with him."

O'Sullivan stared at him, horrified. "A prisoner? Holy Mary Mother of God, what have you done?" It was said in almost a whisper.

O'Sullivan looked up at the sky, slowly shaking his head. For a long moment he didn't move, he just continued to stare upward, then he looked at Carson and said in a low voice, "You son-of-a-bitch. You crazy, self-centered bastard. Do you have any idea what you've done, of what's going to happen to him, an' those other poor souls? No, don't bother to answer, I'll tell you. They are going to die, so they are. But oh what a death, what pain they are goin' to endure.... How many casualties, Captain?"

"Forty-three, in all, sir, including the wounded." Carson lowered his head. "Thirty-two dead, and six missing; five more wounded, not counting me."

"Almost half your bloody command. Well, I hope you can live with yourself, Captain, because I can't."

"Sir, General Sherman's orders were to–"

"I don't give a goddamn what Sherman's orders were. He's not in command here. I am, and you disobeyed my direct order. Lieutenant Daly, you will place this man under arrest, relieve him of his weapons, and send him to the rear of the column under guard. Make sure his wound is seen to. Get him out of my sight, now!"

He didn't bother to watch as Daly escorted Carson along the wadi to the rear of the waiting column. There he detailed two men to escort the captain to the rear of the column.

"Lieutenant Warwick. Take command of what's left of Company G. Take 'em in hand and have 'em fall in at the rear of the column. Consider yourself acting First Lieutenant."

Warwick saluted, gave the order, and did as he was asked.

"Sergeant." O'Sullivan beckoned to one of Carson's, now Warwick's, men as they filed past. The man walked his horse forward to join the group.

"Sergeant, I need you to take us to where this goddamn mess happened, if you can. How long will it take to get us there?"

The man nodded. "I can, Colonel. It's back thataway, maybe a couple of hours, maybe less. We should be there well before dark."

"It's almost four o'clock now," O'Sullivan said, consulting his pocket watch. "It will be dark by eight. If we can get there by six, we'll still have a couple of hours of daylight left. Let's move."

It was just after five-thirty when they arrived at the place where the village had once stood. They came in from the west, slowly, warily. The encampment was deserted, but for the bodies of the dead soldiers, and several dead cavalry horses. The Comanche were gone.

"Where the hell did they go? I wonder," O'Sullivan said, to no one in particular. "Sergeant Major Coffin. Take ten men an' Dahkeya an' go take a look along the riverbank. Don't go too far. Stay within earshot, an' be careful. Keep your wits about you. They may be waitin' for another crack at us.

"Lieutenant Whitworth, same goes for you. Ten men an' Nitis. You go west, beyond the wadi. I don't think you'll find anything, but you never know.

"Lieutenant Daly. You take Bear Claw an' ten men an' scout the perimeter to the north, beyond the trees.

"No more than an hour. I want you back here before dark; no excuses. Is that understood, gentlemen?"

It was, and within a matter of minutes all three scouting parties were on their way.

"Lieutenant Warwick, you detail burial parties. We can't leave these men to the buzzards. See that it's done, and done quickly."

"Yes, sir."

O'Sullivan sat astride his horse and watched as Coffin and his party disappeared into the pass at the eastern end of the valley. He watched, but he didn't see. His mind was elsewhere; he was deep in thought.

Son of a bitch! Where the hell did they go? He twisted in the saddle, his hand on his horse's rump, and he stared up at the mountains to the south. *Nothin' there; no access; sheer rock walls.* He turned in the saddle and looked to the north, took his glasses from the pouch on his saddle, put them to his eyes and scoured the line of

188

trees and the mountains beyond. *Maybe that way. If so, Bear Claw will find sign, I hope.*

He lowered the glasses, held them in both hands, resting them on the pommel of his saddle. Something, it was just a feeling, made him look around to the rear. Some twenty yards away, still on horseback, flanked by two privates, Carson was staring at him, his eyes narrow slits filled with hate.

O'Sullivan turned his horse and walked it back to join him. He reined in his horse a couple of feet in front of Carson, then said to the two guards, "Give us a minute, men. I'll call when I need you." He waited until Carson's guards were out of earshot. "What do you think, Captain?" he asked, waving a hand in the general direction of the place where the dead were being laid to rest. "Proud of yourself?"

Carson didn't answer. He sat still, his hands on the pommel of his saddle, staring stoically head.

"Good men," O'Sullivan said, more to himself than to Carson. "Good men, every one of 'em, an' they died for nothin', so they did. All you had to do was send a rider to me an' then wait. But no, you're so filled with hate an' the desire for revenge you had to go it alone. An' now look at the result: thirty-five good men gone an' soon to be in the ground, an' so far from home their folks'll never know where they are. An' then there's Keogh, an' Jones, an' Kelly. What about them *Captain* Carson? What about them?

189

"Keogh was a mean, evil little bastard, an' maybe he deserved to answer for what you an' he did at Sand Creek, but this.... No, Captain. No one deserves to die the way he's goin' to die. If I could go get him, I would. But there's no way. They're gone, long gone, an' only the Lord knows where. By mornin'.... Well, it don't bear thinkin' about, it don't."

Carson just stared fixedly ahead.

O'Sullivan shook his head, exasperated. Then he waved his hand and beckoned the two guards to return. When they did, he touched his spurs to his horse's flanks and walked him around Carson and slowly back toward the place where the men were digging the single mass grave. The thirty-five bodies, including the three wounded men now dead, were wrapped in blankets and lay in a long line a few yards away from where the men were digging.

O'Sullivan heaved a deep sigh, pulled his glasses from their pouch, and again began to survey the trees and mountains to the north. *Up there. That's where they went. Has to be. They must have a safe haven up there... somewhere.* He lowered the glasses, but continued to stare at up at the distant peaks, tapping the rim of the glasses gently on the pommel of his saddle.

White Eagle and Yellow Crow, high on a crag some half-mile to the north of their abandoned village, stood together and watched the blue coats. A half mile to the south, on a similar high perch, Broken Nose also

190

watched, and to the east two more Comanche warriors also watched.

White Eagle watched through his glasses as the blue coat officer, the Shoshone scout, and their escort threaded their way among the tall pines that hid the arroyo. It would not be long before the cleft between the rock walls was discovered, and then....

He lowered the glasses and looked upward at the darkening sky. The once white clouds, now turned dark gray, were splashed with streaks of red, yellow and orange by the light from the setting sun. Fire in the sky. An omen, perhaps.

He raised the glasses and studied the men in the valley; one in particular caught his eye. The blue coat was obviously their leader, for he sat astride his horse and watched as the men toiled at their work. The blue coat leader had an air about him, and would, White Eagle was sure, be a formidable enemy. He counted their numbers. Including the men in the three small scouting parties, he estimated them to be at least 250 strong. He adjusted the binoculars, refocused them, and trained them again on the blue coat leader. For the first time in his life, he felt unsure.

He turned and spoke to Yellow Crow, who nodded, then turned, and trotted away. White Eagle lifted his hand above his head, turned to the west and signaled Broken Nose to leave his vantage point, then he turned to the north and signaled for the two warriors there to do likewise. He looked once more down into the valley, then turned and walked quickly after Yellow Crow.

It was completely dark when White Eagle and his companions approached the haven, a vast box canyon located in the high mountains some six thousand feet above sea level and almost five miles to the north of the tiny valley they had once called home.

The teepees all had be re-erected. This time, they formed a wide circle, two teepees deep, around a huge fire pit. At first glance, it would appear that the box canyon was not, perhaps, the best place to for the Comanche to take refuge. That glance, however, would be deceiving. Because of the almost sheer rock walls that rose almost vertically for five hundred feet and more, it would be difficult, if not impossible, to evacuate the women and children, should the need arise. White Eagle was no fool, however, and he had chosen this spot with great care.

The approaches to the canyon were wide, perhaps five, even six hundred yards at the mouth, and it looked as if there was no way out. To the rear of the canyon, however, nine hundred, a thousand yards from its entrance, the cliff walls were honeycombed with caves. A half-dozen narrow pathways and trails led upward to the high bluffs above the canyon walls. Those bluffs were inaccessible from outside the canyon. The only way for an invader to reach the heights was via those same trails and paths. It was an imminently defensible, natural citadel. But if he had to get the women and children out.... Only an adequate water supply was missing, which was why White Eagle had not placed his permanent settlement in the canyon. They had been transporting water to the caves continuously for the past two weeks, ever since White Eagle had learned that the blue coats were on the move.

Now, as White Eagle and his companions approached the canyon, they could see the flickering red light of the campfire and hear the steady throb of the drums.

He gave the three prisoners a cursory glance as he swung himself down from his pony, but took little notice of them. He turned the pony over to a small boy, who raced away with him to the far side of the circle, to feed and water him. He looked around the circle, nodded in satisfaction, then turned and entered his teepee where he found Elva sitting beside a small fire.

When White Eagle threw back the flap, she jumped, startled, then rose to her feet and bowed, submissively. He took the four steps to stand in front of, lifted her chin with his forefinger and smiled. "No need you stand like so. You sit. We eat. Yes?"

She nodded, and White Eagle sat, his legs crossed, on the floor by the fire. Using two small sticks, Elva lifted a small earthenware pot from the fire and placed it in front of him. He waited while she lifted a second pot from the fire, set it on the floor, and then sat down.

Together, using wooden spoons, they ate the succulent, stewed buffalo meat. Not a word passed

193

between them until the food was gone. Then White Eagle smacked his lips, wiped his mouth on his forearm, nodded his head, and said, "Good... Elva. Food is good."

She smiled, and they sat for a moment in silence and she looked at him, her face serious. "What will happen to them, the three men?"

His face tightened, and his mouth became a grim thin line. For a moment he didn't reply, then he said, "They die. Tonight."

She nodded, not surprised.

"The one with officer coat. He at Sand Creek. I know him. Him called Kee-oh. He kill women, kill children... take many scalp. The others not at Sand Creek. They die quick, easy. Not him."

Outside, the drums throbbed, the warriors danced around the fire, and chanted. Elva shuddered and hoped that White Eagle would not make her watch.

"We've found it, Colonel," Daly shouted as he rode at the canter into the clearing, followed by Bear Claw and the troopers.

"What? You found what? Where?" O'Sullivan was infected by Daly's enthusiasm.

"There's an arroyo, a gorge, back there, beyond the trees. And there's sign, lots of it."

"Where? Show me?"

It took but a few minutes for Daly and Bear Claw to take O'Sullivan through the trees to the mouth of the arroyo. At first, he couldn't see it. Even when they had approached to within only a few yards, he could still barely make out the entrance to the gorge, so well hidden was it by the natural rock formations that surrounded it.

Beyond the gap, the way forward opened up and became yet another dry riverbed that seemed to meander northward and upward, bordered on either side by towering cliffs, sheer rock faces topped by junipers, bristlecone, and mountain maple.

"Well," O'Sullivan said, glancing up at the darkening sky. "It will have to wait until daylight. Even then, this place will be a death trap. Couldn't pick a better place for an ambush m'self. We'll wait until daybreak, then come an' take a look see. Let's head back. There's no point in temptin' 'em, right?"

Daly agreed, and the three men turned their horses and headed back through the trees. Deep within the canyon, a single coyote howled, and O'Sullivan shuddered, involuntarily.

Chapter 22

White Eagle's Village, August 24, Evening

The great fire blazed and cast huge shadows onto the canyon wall, turning it into a wildly undulating nightmare world of heaving black monsters, set against a fiery red flickering backdrop. Lieutenant Keogh, spread-eagled on a huge, wooden X-shaped cross a few feet from the fire, hung listless from his bonds. He was naked, the broken shaft of the arrow that had brought him down still protruding from his chest. He was all but unconscious.

On either side of him, the two troopers, Jones and Kelly were tied to stakes. Kelly was already beyond feeling his pain. The Minnie ball in his upper abdomen had wreaked havoc with his internal organs. His time left was short. Trooper Jones, wounded by an arrow to his left shoulder blade, still had plenty of life left in him, and he was staring wildly around the encampment.

For several hours after darkness had fallen, the drums throbbed. The elders of the band, the women, and even small children watched the gyrations of the warriors until, just before midnight, White Eagle, in full regalia, stepped out of his teepee and into the firelight.

Yellow Crow and Broken Nose each took up station behind the two troopers.

White Eagle stood for several moments, surveying the scene in front of him, then he walked forward a few feet, and raised both arms high above his head. His bare chest glistened in the light of the flickering flames. The streaks of black war paint looked like jagged wounds across his face and torso.

The drums stopped, the dancing warriors came to a halt and stood stiff and still around the great fire.

White Eagle lowered his arms, walked a few feet to stand in front of the tribal elders and began to speak. His voice was soft, almost lilting, but as the speech continued, it became louder and angrier. The chief punctuated his words with violent hand gestures, most of them in the direction of now wide-awake Lieutenant Keogh.

Finally, the speech was over. For several moments, the elders conversed quietly among themselves. Then, the oldest of them looked up at White Eagle and nodded.

White Eagle smiled, a terrible grim smile. He turned and walked around the fire to stand in front of Keogh. "Now, Kee-oh, the elders of the Kwahadi have spoken. It is time for you to pay for what you did at Sand Creek."

If he could have, Keogh would had stood defiantly upright and stared the chief in the eye, but bound as he was to the X-shaped cross, all he could do was hold his head upright and glare at him.

"Go to hell you stinkin' savage. You think this is it? No it ain't. Go ahead, kill me. That Irish bastard will soon be here, an' he'll send you, an' your stinkin' tribe o' savages straight to hell." He tried to spit in White eagle's

197

face, but his mouth was dry, and what little saliva he could muster fell well short.

"Yes, Kee-oh. I will kill you. But you will know such pain as no man has ever known." White Eagle drew his knife from its sheath on his belt and nodded to Yellow Crow and Broken Nose. They both stepped forward and grabbed both troopers by the hair, pulling their heads back against the stakes. Reaching around, they slashed their throats, and then stepped back. Kelly felt no pain; he was already too far gone. For him, it was a quick release. His head fell forward onto his chest and within seconds he was dead. Jones coughed once, opened his mouth and tried to scream, but no sound came out. His head fell forward, and his life blood ran down his chest and pooled at his feet.

Keogh continued to stare defiantly at White Eagle, then closed his eyes, smiled, and waited.

White Eagle stepped forward and, with a single, back-handed swipe of his knife, slashed Keogh's chest from his right shoulder almost to the left side of his waist. For a moment, Keogh felt nothing... and then his scream echoed and reechoed around the walls of the canyon.

Chapter 23

Box Canyon, August 25

The troopers rose early the following morning. The night had been uneventful, but few among the more than 250 troops of the command had gotten much sleep.

As soon as it was light enough to see, O'Sullivan, his senior officers and Coffin, along with Bear Claw, the two Apache scouts and a small escort of troopers, left the lakeside camp and headed north through the tall pines to reconnoiter the gorge, White Eagle's escape route.

"How long, Bear Claw? How many?" O'Sullivan reined his horse to a stop, swung his left leg over its ears and dropped easily to the ground. They were perhaps a half mile into the gorge.

Bear Claw also dismounted. For several moments, he walked the canyon floor, stopping now and then, stooping to pick up something, or to run his fingers through the fine sand that covered the ground. Then he returned to where O'Sullivan and the others were waiting.

"Many ponies. Many peoples. Not more than two days. Two hundred, maybe many more. Horses with steel feet, ponies... maybe 120... 150 ponies, many women, children, walking, see, there...." He pointed to the imprints in the sand, many of them made by small feet.

O'Sullivan nodded and walked a few yards on up the wadi, his hands on his hips, his head tilted back, staring upward at the high bluffs. He seemed to make up his mind about something, then he turned and walked quickly back to his horse. "We'll head back, get something to eat, assemble the command, an' then get after 'em. Let's go."

Back at the encampment, the men were already making ready to leave. The tents had been taken down, folded, and loaded onto the pack animals. Captain Morgan was overseeing the loading of his guns and ammunition onto the mules, and the fires were being put out.

"Not so fast, Sergeant," O'Sullivan said to the man in charge of dowsing the last of the fires. "We need breakfast, so we do. Get that fire going again and have someone cook up some bacon, beans and coffee, an' I'll have a slice or two fried bread to go with mine."

He swung himself down from his horse, handed him off to one of the troopers who had been clearing the site, and then settled himself down on a log to wait.

"You gentlemen will join me," he said, looking up at Daly, Warwick, Morgan, Whitworth, and Coffin. "How is *Mr.* Carson doin' this fine mornin', Sergeant Major?"

"*Mr.* Carson is doing fine, Colonel. Still under guard, an' as ornery as a stuck pig, but he's doin' fine."

"All right then," O'Sullivan said, looking around the now seated group. Despite all that had happened the previous day, his mood was optimistic. "The sun is shinin' an' it's goin' to be a beautiful day. What do you think, Captain Morgan? Can we get the guns up there, or will we leave 'em here?"

"Well, it won't be easy, and it will be slow going, but it can be done. We'll need to rest the animals, often, but it can be done."

"So be it, then. We'll leave in half an hour. Now let's eat. I'm bloody starvin', so I am. Gimme some o' that coffee, Sergeant."

It was more than a half hour before they were able to get moving, but by ten o'clock the entire command had moved into the gorge and was making its way slowly, two abreast, along the dry riverbed.

As Captain Morgan had thought, the going was tough, especially for the mules carrying the guns. The mountain howitzer had been designed to be packed over such rough country, but this rocky riverbed was not quite what its designers had in mind.

The howitzer's big brother, the twelve-pounder Napoleon smoothbore field gun, had a tube that weighed over 1200 pounds. It's carriage weighed more than 1100 and the combined gun required six draft horses to pull it around. In comparison, the tube of the twelve-pounder mountain howitzer gun tube was half as long as that of the Napoleon and weighed a mere 220 pounds, no more than a good-sized man, thus it was easily carried by a big, strong mule. The howitzer's carriage weighed a hundred pounds and each wheel was just sixty-five pounds, making the total weight of the mountain howitzer a little more than five hundred pounds in all, thus each gun required a team of three mules to transport it. The ammunition was carried by four more mules. Even so, the steep terrain and the uneven surface of the riverbed required that the mules be rested every hour. By one o'clock, the command had traveled a paltry three miles, and, as far as O'Sullivan could tell, there was no end in sight.

Just after they had negotiated a particularly tight bend in the gorge, Coffin spotted something four or five hundred yards ahead in the center of the wadi beside a large juniper tree.

It was difficult to make it out. The thing, whatever it was, shapeless and shimmered in the heat of the midday sun, surrounded by a glittering, silver outline.

"Look." Coffin grabbed O'Sullivan's arm. "There up ahead, by the tree."

"What the hell is that?" Daly stared at the apparition.

O'Sullivan dragged his glasses from their pouch and put them to his eyes. "Cain't tell. The light is too bright. Move on. We'll need to get closer."

It wasn't until they were within twenty yards or so, that, almost as one, they realized what they were looking at.

"That," Coffin said, grimly, "was, Lieutenant Keogh."

"Holy Mother," O'Sullivan said, quickly crossing himself. "What the hell did they do to him? Halt the column, Lieutenant Daly. Have 'em stay back; they don't need to see this."

He swung himself out of the saddle and walked the few yards to where the blackened, mortal remains of what once had been Lieutenant Keogh stared through empty eye sockets down the riverbed toward them. Even for O'Sullivan, after four terrible years of civil war, it was a sight beyond comprehension.

Keogh's naked, broken burned body had been tied to a stake set in a pile of loose rocks in the center of the riverbed. A rope tied around his forehead held his head upright against the stake. The broken shaft of an arrow still protruded from his chest, just below his right shoulder. His chest had been slashed, crisscrossed with deep knife wounds. His eyes and nose were gone - taken by predatory birds; his teeth smiled out from his lipless mouth. His arms hung by his sides. His hands were little more than blacked stubs, fingers charred to the bones, blackened sticks curled like the claws of some demonic cat. His genitals....

"Sergeant Major Coffin," O'Sullivan shouted. "Get some men. Cut him down. Wait! Before you cut him down, I want.... My God. Jesus Christ...." It appeared for a moment that he was going to throw up, but he didn't. He walked back to his horse. "Lieutenant Daly. Please go to the rear and bring forward *Mr.* Carson."

Daly did as he was asked. O'Sullivan leaned against his horse and waited, his head buried in the crook of his arms against the animal's flank.

Daly, along with Carson and his escort, arrived just a couple of moments later. Carson sat in the saddle and stared stoically at his one-time second in command, but not for long. Two huge hands grasped his right arm and dragged him bodily from the back of the horse. He crashed to ground, landing hard on his back, the breath driven from his body. In an instant, O'Sullivan sat astride him, his hands tight around his throat, his fingers squeezing.

"You goddamn piece o' horseshit," O'Sullivan snarled through gritted teeth, screwing his thumbs into Carson's neck. "I'm gonna send you straight to hell where you belong."

Carson's face was already turning blue when Coffin and Daly managed, with great difficulty, to drag him off and away from the struggling captain.

O'Sullivan sat on the ground, growling something to himself that none but he could understand. His hat had fallen off, his face was bright red, and spittle ran from the corners of his mouth. Never, in all the years Coffin had known O'Sullivan, had he seen him so enraged. But it wasn't yet over. O'Sullivan scrambled to his knees and dived at the still gasping, winded Carson.

Before he could reach him, Daly grabbed his arm and spun him around. Coffin dived on O'Sullivan's back, wrapped his arms around his neck and wrestled him to the ground, then lay across his chest, holding him down.

To the rear, the leading ranks of the column watched in awe. To see one officer strike another was unheard of, to watch one commit murder was....

"Bloody hell, Ronan," Coffin yelled in O'Sullivan's ear. "Stop it, for Christ's sake. You'll kill him."

"Bloody right I will," O'Sullivan shouted, struggling to throw Coffin off. "I'll send that piece o' shit direc'ly to his master in hell, so I will. Lemme go, dammit. I'm gonna kill 'im.

But Coffin didn't let go. "Get him outa here," he yelled at Daly.

Daly, not sure of what to do about Coffin, had Carson's escort pick him up and take him to the rear. He went, staggering, doubled over, coughing and spluttering, mumbling inaudibly to himself.

Then Daly put a hand on Coffin's shoulder. "Sergeant Major Coffin, you'd better...."

"It's all right, Lieutenant Daly," Coffin said, twisting his to look up at him. "I've got him. He be all right. Just give me a minute to calm him down."

And slowly, O'Sullivan did calm down, and Coffin climbed off his chest. O'Sullivan rose unsteadily to his feet, looked around for his hat, picked it up, dusted it off, put it on, and pulled the brim down over his eyes. Then he dusted himself off, adjusted his uniform jacket, and looked around with a sheepish grin.

"Well," he said. "They'll pull me rank for that one, that's for sure, an' bloody good riddance to it, too." Then he glanced at what remained of Keogh and sadly shook his head. "Cut the poor bugger down. Bury him over there, somewhere." He pointed toward the rock wall. "He was a mean son of a bitch, an' he did some terrible things, but he didn't deserve to die like that, nobody does."

Keogh was duly buried under a pile of rocks, and Daly, hat in hand, not knowing what else to say over the grave, simply said, "Rest in peace, Lieutenant Ewan Keogh, rest in peace."

They mounted up, and O'Sullivan cast a glance along the long line of the command, nodded his head, and said to Coffin, "You'd better go take a look at Carson, an' make sure he's still kickin', I s'pose."

Coffin returned a few minutes later and nodded at O'Sullivan, who smiled back at him, and said, "Hah! I must be loosin' it. Time was I would've broke his bloody neck, instead all I managed to was choke the bugger a little."

He reached inside his coat, pulled out his pocket watch, flipped it open, took note of the time, then waved the column forward. It was just after two o'clock in the afternoon. They reached the mouth of the box canyon two hours later.

O'Sullivan called a halt at the mouth of the canyon. He had an uneasy feeling that he was being watched, the feeling so strong his skin crawled. He reached for his binoculars, put them to his eyes, and surveyed the Comanche campsite, the rock walls, and peaks and ridges high above. Nothing, at least nothing he could see.

"They're there," he said, to no one in particular. "They have to be. Where would they go? There's no way out, that I can see. There's some caves, in the far wall, but...."

The inner canyon did indeed appear to be deserted. All that was left of the campfire were the still smoldering embers and a few wisps of smoke. The teepees, too, were deserted, at least far as O'Sullivan could tell. For several minutes, he continued to scour the deepest reaches of the canyon. All was quiet. Then, CRACK! A single shot rang out, the report echoing around and off of the canyon walls. The heavy Minnie ball slammed into the dirt between O'Sullivan's horse's front feet, throwing up a fountain of dust and splinters of rock, causing the startled animal to rear and twist and try to run. O'Sullivan almost fell, but managed somehow to hang on and then control the panicking beast.

"Take cover," he yelled, backing the horse away along the draw until they were out of sight.

For several moments, he sat, waiting. Nothing.

"Sergeant Major, Mr. Daly, Bear Claw. With me," he called over his shoulder. "The rest of you stay here an' keep out of sight."

He waited for the two men and the scout to join him, then touched his spurs to the horse's flanks and walked him slowly forward until he could again see into the canyon. He raised his glasses and peered through them. Nothing was moving, not even the air. The heat was oppressive. He ranged his glasses back and forth, searching the ridges and bluffs. Still nothing. Then he saw them, three small figures outlined against the deep blue of the sky. So high up were they that they appeared tiny to the naked eye. Through the glasses, however, O'Sullivan could see that all three were armed with rifles, though what sort he couldn't tell. One of them wore the feathered headdress of a chief.

So there you are.

"Up there, just above that crest, to the left, there, see?" He handed Coffin the glasses.

"I see 'em," Daly said. He had his own glasses to his eyes.

"Bear Claw?" O'Sullivan said.

"White Eagle, and... I look?" Bear Claw held out his hand, and O'Sullivan passed the binoculars to him.

Bear Claw nodded. "White Eagle, Yellow Crow and one I do not know." He handed the glasses back to O'Sullivan.

"Do you know him? White Eagle?" O'Sullivan asked. "Will he talk to you?"

"I know him, and Yellow Crow. Talk? Maybe, maybe not."

"Oh, he wants to talk all right," O'Sullivan said. "I would be dead by now if he didn't, so I would. He put

208

that shot exactly where he wanted it to go, a message to get our attention. Go get Dahkeya and Nitis," he said to Bear Claw, "an' go into the canyon under a white flag. Let's see what he wants, if anythin'."

"You think he'll honor a white flag?" Coffin asked. "He ain't nothin' but a savage."

Bear Claw looked sharply at Coffin, and said, "Not savage. White Eagle honorable chief of Kwahadi Comanche. He will respect flag."

"Geeze." Coffin shook his head. "Better you than me, an' good luck to you."

Five minutes later, Bear Claw, Dahkeya, and Nitis walked their horses slowly forward into the canyon. Bear Claw had a white shirt tied to the barrel of his rifle, its butt set against the left side of his hip.

O'Sullivan watched the three men on the ridge top pull back out of sight, and he smiled. *He'll talk, so he will.*

White Eagle, Yellow Crow, Broken Nose and three warriors watched for several moments as the three scouts entered the canyon and made their way slowly toward the north end. Finally, when he was satisfied that the three men were alone, he nodded to his two companions, then nudged his pony forward and they made their way down the mountain to meet them.

O'Sullivan and Daly watched through their glasses as the chief and the Shoshone scout spoke animatedly, their hands moving in sharp, jerking motions to emphasize important points in the exchange. White

Eagle was obviously angry, but Bear Claw held his own, and was just as animated as the chief. Finally, the two groups turned their mounts away from each other. The Comanche galloped away to the rear, the scouts returned to O'Sullivan at a much more leisurely pace.

"What did he have to say? Will he talk to me?" O'Sullivan asked.

"Not talk, Colonel. He will listen to what you have to say, but he says you must leave this place or many blue coats will die. You, me, and two more can go. He will meet you, there." Bear Claw pointed to a pair of old-growth junipers some fifty yards into the canyon. "We go, now."

"Mr. Warwick. Bring forward a detachment and have them line up back there, just beyond those rocks. Stay on the alert. Watch for my, or Mr. Daly's, signal. If either of us gives that signal, have men bring their arms to bear, but *do not* fire unless I give the word. Do you understand, Lieutenant?"

"I do, Colonel. On orders from you or Lieutenant Daly I am to bring weapons to bear, but we are not to fire unless you, yourself, give the word."

"Correct, Lieutenant. Now go to it, an' quickly. Mr. Daly, Sergeant Major, you are with me. Bear Claw, you may lead the way."

The four men walked their horses slowly forward. O'Sullivan and Coffin were both visibly nervous, eyes darting, scouring the terrain for signs of trouble. Daly, experienced as he was with Indians, not so much. When they reached the two trees, they stopped, and waited. There was no sign of White Eagle.

For almost ten minutes they waited, and then they appeared.

White Eagle was mounted on an all-black pony and dressed in the regalia of a principle chief of the Comanche Nation: full headdress complete with a train of red and white feathers that extended down his back. Had he been on foot, it would reached almost to his ankles. His face was streaked with black war paint, three stripes on either cheek that extended from the bridge of his nose to his jaw. His chest was bare and also streaked with black paint. His legs were bare, he wore no leggings, just a leather breechcloth. He, too, carried a white flag. It was attached to the tip of his war lance; the steel point glistened in the sunlight.

Slowly, and with great dignity, the three Comanche rode toward them until they reached a spot some ten yards from where O'Sullivan and his companions were waiting. They stopped, White Eagle in the center and slightly forward of the other two. They sat still, their backs rigid, White Eagle with the butt end of the lance resting on his right foot, the other two with the butts of their rifles resting on their thighs.

For several moments, both parties sat and stared at each other; not a word passed between them.

"Tell him my name is Lieutenant Colonel O'Sullivan. I am here to talk of peace with him."

Bear Claw spoke rapidly, punctuating his words with short, sharp hand gestures. White Eagle spat, said just one word to the scout, and then stared O'Sullivan directly in the eye, his gaze unflinching.

Bear Claw tried again. White Eagle did not reply; he continued to stare at O'Sullivan.

"He will not speak to you," Bear Claw said.

O'Sullivan turned to Bear Claw. "Tell him we mean him no harm. Tell him... Tell him... I killed the gray coat soldiers, and–"

"I speak English, white man," the chief snarled, interrupting him. "You tell me."

O'Sullivan was taken aback, but quickly recovered. "I am here to talk peace with you, White Eagle. Your people are suffering. I can help you put a stop to it."

"You are blue coat *nantan*?"

O'Sullivan looked at Bear Claw. "Nantan?"

"Comanche word for chief."

O'Sullivan nodded. "Yes, I am nantan. I command these soldiers. Will you talk peace with me?"

"Your words of peace mean nothing. Too long have Comanche suffered at white man's hands. Blue coats kill women, children; white men take our lands. Plains, mountains," he swept his hand in a wide circle, "our lands. Comanche here before steel hats come. Now blue coats, white men, steal all land, kill Comanche, kill Cheyenne, Arapaho, Apache; kill buffalo."

O'Sullivan looked round at Daly. "Steel hats?"

"The Spanish Conquistadores."

O'Sullivan nodded, then turned again to face the Comanche chief. "What you say is true, White Eagle, but the killing has to stop. You are fighting a war you cannot win. If you don't give yourselves up, we will hunt you down, an' blue coats like Keogh, not me, will kill you an' your people, all of them. An' you know that what I say is true. If you didn't, you would not be talkin' to me."

White Eagle stared at him, his eyed narrowed, and then he said, "White Eagle not start killing. First, gray coat soldiers come, kill my son, his wife, and child. Then Nantan Chiv-in'-ton, Kee-oh, and many more blue coats kill women, children at Sand Creek – Ayasha, my daughter... she woman of Arapaho warrior, dead, scalped... Kee-oh did this. Now Kee-oh dead."

"Yes, I know. We found him a ways back down the canyon. That was quite a job you did on him. Where are my other two men?"

"They are dead. They die quick. No pain. My people bury them in the canyon."

O'Sullivan stared at the chief, his lips a thin a line. For almost a minute, the two men sat staring at each other, their eyes locked together, then O'Sullivan nodded. There was nothing he could say, nothing worth saying.

"I know about the gray coats, White Eagle, an' I know what they did to your people. I know they killed your ponies. I killed them, all of them. An' I know what

213

happened at Sand Creek, an' I promise it will not happen again."

"You promise. Hah! How you promise? White men destroy everything, *everything*," White Eagle snarled. "Buffalo; white men kill all buffalo. They kill for skins, not food. Soon buffalo gone from plains. What Comanche, Cheyenne, Apache, all, eat when buffalo gone, blue coat? You feed us? Hah! You are funny man, Nantan Oh-sull-van. The land groans under white man's feet." He stared at O'Sullivan, slowly shaking his head.

"Yes, White Eagle. The army will make sure you are well fed, have land to hunt the buffalo, and live in peace with the white man.

"I am authorized to offer you amnesty for... well, for what you have done in the past, safe haven, good land, lots of land, in Colorado Territory, but you must come in with me, an' you must turn over your captives, the Bryson family an' the woman you took from Newsom's Station. No harm will come to you, or your people. I give you my word."

"How can you give me what is already mine? A thousand summers my people have been here. Then you come. Take land. Steal land. Now you say you give back what is already mine. Hah!

"Your word, blue coat, is like the wind that blows through mountains; it change from one day to next. Nantan Wynkoop also give word, to Black Kettle, and many Black Kettle peoples die. Blue coat word mean *nothing* to White Eagle." He spat the words out, his face an angry mask. He turned to Yellow Crow, muttering something O'Sullivan did not understand. Yellow Crow stared at O'Sullivan, his eyes mere slits among the war paint.

"We go now, Oh-sull-van. You not follow." White Eagle lifted the lance from his foot, spun it between his fingers, then hurled it, point down, the white flag still attached, into the ground at his pony's feet. The pony, startled by the sudden movement, reared, but White Eagle had him under control and turned him again to face O'Sullivan.

He pointed at the lance now stuck solidly in the dirt. "Do not pass. If you do... you die." He swung his pony around and, followed by Yellow Crow and Broken Nose, trotted away toward the rear of the canyon.

"Wait." O'Sullivan turned and shouted.

"Lieutenant Daly."

"Ready!" Daly shouted, and fifty rifles were raised and aimed at White Eagle and his companions.

"What's to stop me from taking you now, White Eagle? You an' these two men?" O'Sullivan asked.

White Eagle turned his pony to face him. He said nothing. He simply smiled at O'Sullivan, raised his head slightly and looked up at the bluffs high above them to the right and pointed. Then he turned his head, looked at those to the right, and again pointed. On both sides of the canyon, more than a hundred of his warriors lined the cliff tops, their weapons trained on the soldiers below.

"No, you tell me, blue coat. What stop me from killing all you... now?" Still smiling he turned again, touched his heels to his pony's flanks, and, without looking back, walked him slowly away into the canyon, followed by Yellow Crow and Broken Nose.

"I cannot leave, White Eagle," O'Sullivan called after him. "If you will not come in with me, I must take you by force. We must fight, an' many men will die. You cannot escape. There's no way out of there."

"Then they must die, Oh-sull-van," White Eagle called back over his shoulder. "Your soldiers and mine. You have no way in, no way to the high ground. That is mine. Go away, Oh-sull-van, and I will let you live."

They watched him go, then O'Sullivan turned and said, "Have the men lower their weapons, Mr. Daly."

Daly did as he was asked. The men lowered their rifles, and all of them remained still until White Eagle had disappeared from sight. O'Sullivan looked up at the high ridges; the warriors were gone.

Chapter 24

White Eagle's Village, August 25

Earlier that morning, White Eagle made plans for the safety of his people. It was too late to completely evacuate the village, but he had known this when they left the valley; the blue coats were too close. But the canyon was a natural, if inverted fortress.

"You must go into the caves, Elva. The blue coat soldiers come. Perhaps we fight. I not able to get all Kwahadi away from this place before they come. You take... Dora and small ones. You be safe in caves 'till blue coats gone. Then we find new place, new home."

"They will kill you, White Eagle. You cannot beat them. They have just fought a great war. They know how to win."

"This place," he waved his arm in a circle, pointing to the mountain tops, "they cannot reach. Only way up is paths, there." Again he pointed. "We will be there, high, on mountain. They die here, below." He nodded his head to emphasize the point. "You go now, to cave, take Dora. Blue coat soldiers soon leave. Then we go, too."

Elva looked at him and shook her head. For some reason she could not fathom, she felt sorry for this man who thought he could fight the U.S. Army and win. She also knew that the caves would not be safe, but she

217

nodded her head and went to find Dora Bryant and the children.

Together, the two women grabbed a water jug, some scraps of food, and several skins to soften the rock floor of the cave. Then they made their way slowly up the narrow path to the caves and the ridge-tops beyond. And there they settled down to wait.

By five o'clock that same afternoon, White Eagle had all of his warriors spread out along the tops of ridges all along the canyon. He had almost 150 of them up there, some more than six hundred feet above the canyon floor. Almost half of them were armed with a diversity of rifles, including twenty-nine Sharps carbines and fourteen Spencer repeating rifles. There were also more than a dozen Springfield muzzleloaders, two Whitworths, several Lorenz rifles, a couple of Frank Wesson rifles, and even a Sharps & Hankins carbine, a model made exclusively for the U.S. Navy. A few were armed with handguns, the rest with bows and arrows.

Now, they lay in wait, well hidden behind the high ridges and escarpments, the floor of the box canyon spread out before them. White Eagle was more than satisfied with his commanding position. Even at extreme range, the mouth of the canyon was no more than eight hundred yards away. If the blue coats advanced into the canyon, as he hoped they would, they would be easy targets, even for the bowmen. For the warriors armed with rifles.... He smiled at the thought.

From the mouth of the canyon, O'Sullivan, Daly, Morgan, Coffin, and the rest of the officers sat astride their horses and surveyed the interior, the walls, and the ridges that surrounded them on three sides. As far as any of them could tell, the village was deserted. Where they had all gone, none of them could guess. Though he couldn't see them, O'Sullivan was sure White Eagle and his men were hidden and lying in wait on the heights. The ponies, those they could see, were corralled beneath the rock wall at the right side of the canyon.

"What do you think, Mr. Daly?" O'Sullivan asked. "They're waitin' for us, up there, among the ridges, wouldn't you agree?"

"Either that or they're gone; high-tailed it outa here."

"Nope. Not him. That one's gonna fight this time, so he is. What about it, Boone? Any ideas?"

"No, Colonel, not a one. I'll leave the thinkin' all to you, but I'm thinkin' maybe...."

"You an' me both, which is why I brought 'em along. Captain Morgan. Bring up the guns, if you will. How long until you can get 'em ready for action?"

"Not long, Colonel. Thirty minutes, maybe thirty-five. We have to unload 'em from the mules an' assemble the carriages, and—"

"Twenty minutes, Mr. Morgan; twenty minutes. There's only a couple of hours of daylight left, an' I want this done an' over with before it gets dark."

Morgan flipped him a somewhat sloppy salute, wheeled his horse, and galloped toward the rear, shouting orders as he went.

"I think," O'Sullivan said, to no one in particular, "that me fine-feathered friend is in for something of a shock. Wouldn't you agree, Lieutenant Daly? I wonder if he has any idea what we have in store for him."

"I should think not, Colonel. He wouldn't have waited around if he had."

It took Captain Morgan and his two gun crews only nineteen minutes to get the two howitzers off the mules and into their carriages. He bustled around them, inspecting everything, made a few final adjustments, and then turned his attention to the ammunition. When he was done, he walked the few yards back to where O'Sullivan and his entourage were still sitting, watching for any signs of movement on the ridges or in the canyon. There were none.

"All ready, Colonel," Morgan said, looking up at him. "Where would you like me to put 'em?"

"Hahaha, that's quite a question, so it is, Captain. Where would I like you to put 'em indeed. No, never mind. Bring 'em forward, if you will, but for God's sake try an' stay out of sight. I don't want 'em to know what we're up to until we're ready. Place one there." He pointed to spot he'd picked out earlier at the left side of the canyon mouth, well hidden, so he hoped, behind several creeping juniper bushes. "An' the other one over there." Again, he pointed to a similar spot, this time to the right.

"Now, me fine friend." He grinned at Captain Morgan. "Those hammers of yours, can you elevate them so they can reach the tops of the ridges?"

"I can, an' higher, if need be."

"So then, you range the right-hand gun to the left, and the one on the left to the right. Can you see through those bloody bushes? What would be the range, do you think?"

Morgan stared at the ridges, contemplating. "Eight hundred yards, maybe a tad more, an' yes, I can see, an' fire through the bushes, if need be."

O'Sullivan nodded. "It need be, Captain Morgan, it need be indeed. Load 'em with Hotchkiss and make ready to fire, but not until I give you the target."

Elva, from her vantage point at the cave entrance halfway up the cliff face, lay on her stomach, Dora Bryson, beside her. She looked out over and along the canyon toward its entrance. She could see very little, the distance was too great, and whatever the blue coats were up to, they staying well hidden while they did it.

She scanned the ridgetops. Nothing. Wherever White Eagle was, she couldn't see. She was worried. She knew that the Comanche had little to no chance of winning a toe-to-toe battle with the well-armed soldiers.

She turned, walked into the cave, and sat down beside Dora and the two children, both of whom were scared, crying, and cuddled up against their mother. She reached out and stroked the littlest girl's hair, and, for a moment, she quieted down and looked up at Elva, her eyes filled with tears.

"Dora, you must stay here in the cave, no matter what happens. The soldiers are doing something, I don't know what, at the mouth of the canyon. It will be dark in a couple of hours, but I think this will all be over by then. We just have to be patient and stay safe."

Dora nodded. "What will happen to us if he is whipped? Will the Indians kill us?"

"No, White Eagle is many things, but he doesn't kill women and children. Only we do that, well, some of us. No, if we stay here, we'll be safe enough, and the soldiers will rescue us.

At that moment, White Eagle swept into the cave. He stood at the entrance, his form dark, outlined by backlight. It was a fearsome apparition, and both of the little ones screamed at the sight.

"Elva, Dora. Blue coat soldiers soon come. You stay here. When sun sets, when sky is dark, I come for you. We leave here."

He didn't wait for an answer. He left the cave and ran quickly up the narrow path to the top of the bluff on the left side of the canyon. Elva watched until he was out of sight, and then rejoined the Brysons. Together they all moved deeper into the cave and settled down to wait.

The children huddled against their mother, wrapped in her skirts.

When White Eagle arrived on top of the ridge, Yellow Crow was waiting for him and handed him his Spencer rifle. Together, the chiefs walked the battle line of warriors. All were well hidden behind what could only be called a row of natural battlements. Like some medieval castle, the high ridges offered deep cover, thick rock walls, vast boulders, crags, nooks, and crannies. Natural openings offered hidden vantage points and uninterrupted fields of fire over the canyon floor. It was a good position, and White Eagle was well pleased.

He put his glasses to his eyes and surveyed the far end of the canyon where he knew the blue coats must be preparing to attack. He wasn't worried. They could not reach the heights. It would be impossible as long as he held them. He had enough warriors and ammunition, and could, he was certain, hold them indefinitely. He could slowly whittle away at the numbers of the soldiers until they must give up and go away.

And then he saw something, a flash of movement beyond the mouth of the canyon. What it was, he couldn't tell, but the blue coats were busy. White Eagle looked up at the sky. The sun was still high above the ridges to the west. It would be two hours before it sank behind the far mountains. No matter, let them come.

Yellow Crow nudged him and pointed, startling him out of his reverie.

At the far end of the canyon, a large troop of blue coat soldiers came hurtling toward them. At full gallop, dust and rocks flying from the horse's hooves, they charged. White Eagle waved both hands in the air, pulling the trigger of the Spencer in his right hand as he did so, giving the signal for his warriors to open fire.

All along the top of the gorge, his warriors opened fire with rifle and bow, but to no avail. They had been taken by surprise by the speeding blue coats and were moving too fast to target. In seconds, they were out of the saddle and had taken cover, and were quickly returning fire. The hail of lead from the center of the valley floor was intimidating, though it did little harm. His men stayed well hidden, and though they were soon being bombarded by shards of rock and pulverized lead, they were able to return fire without exposing themselves to direct fire.

It was, White Eagle knew, no more than a ruse to flush them out into the open. He smiled. If Oh-sull-van thought he could... well, the man was a fool.

Some thirty minutes earlier, as Captain Morgan put his guns into battery....

"*Mr. Warwick*," O'Sullivan shouted. "To me, if you please."

Warwick came forward at the rush and saluted.

O'Sullivan returned his salute. "Now then *First* Lieutenant." Warwick grinned at him. "I have a very important task for you, so I do.

224

"I want you to take thirty men, weapons cocked an' ready to fire, an' I want you ride, hell for leather, hard as you can, into the canyon, to those rocks over there, about a hundred yards away. Then you'll leap down from your mounts like the divil is after you, take cover an' start pourin' fire up at those ridges an' don't stop whatever happens. Have you got it?"

"Yessir, thirty men, rocks, fire at the ridges; got it."

"Good. Now go to it.

Warwick ran toward the rear.

"Mr. Morgan, Mr. Daly, Sergeant Major Coffin. As soon as the boy opens fire, I want you to keep your eyes peeled for our feathered friend. I want to know exactly where he's hidin', an' then I'll hand 'im the surprise of his life.

"Now then, Lieutenant Daly, you keep an eye on the left side, I'll watch the right; we'll both watch the ridges at the end of the canyon. You spot White Eagle, you let me know."

Five minutes later, Lieutenant Warwick, followed by thirty troopers, all yelling and hollering, tore past the position where O'Sullivan, Daly and Coffin were scouring the battlements for any signs of movement.

The minute Warwick and his men burst out into the open and onto the canyon floor, they were met by a hail of Minnie balls and arrows from above on both sides of the rift. But they were moving too fast, and most of the balls and arrows fell long, behind them. Even before the horses had skittered to a long sliding stop, the troopers

225

were out of the saddle and rolling for cover. Not a single one was hit. As soon as they found cover, they opened up on the heights. The repeating rifles sent a hail of lead upward into the rocks and ridges.

O'Sullivan, Daly, and Coffin searched the skyline for the feathered headdress. Nothing. All around the top of the canyon, now ringed with gray-white smoke, the muzzle flashes of the Comanche rifles lit up the late afternoon skyline. For almost ten minutes, Warwick's troopers kept up their steady rate of fire. The ear-shattering noise of the sustained gunfire within the confines of box canyon was palpable, unimaginable in its volume. It echoed and reverberated around and off the walls, as if the very ground was shaking.

Of White Eagle, there was no sign.

Well now, it doesn't look like Mr. Warwick can flush him out. "MR. MORGAN! To me, if you please."

Morgan spun on his heel and ran the few yards from the gun he had been adjusting. "Sir!"

"I have two targets for you, Captain," he shouted through cupped hand in order to be heard over the roar of the gunfire in the canyon. "See that knob up there to the left?" He pointed upward.

"I do."

"An' to the right, that narrow cleft, almost at the end of the canyon?"

"Yes, Colonel."

"One round each, Hotchkiss. Put 'em, if you can, onto the rock face, fifteen, maybe twenty feet down from the top. I want you to blow the hell out of the canyon wall. Can you do that?"

"With pleasure, Colonel."

"On my mark, then, Captain. Go to it."

Morgan ran first to the gun on the right, sighted along the barrel at the left side of the canyon, found the rocky knob, realigned the gun just a little, adjusted the elevating screw slightly, nodded to himself, then ran to the second gun and went through the same ritual. Finally, he stood upright, turned to face O'Sullivan, and held up his hand to indicate that he was ready. O'Sullivan nodded, and Morgan dropped his hand.

BAM, BAM! The two guns roared almost together. They reared almost two feet into the air. Great plumes of red fire and blue-white smoke belched from their muzzles. Then they slammed down again onto their wheels.

The three men on horseback watched as the shells arched upward toward the ridges. The hang time was less than four seconds until they smashed into the rock walls and exploded in a vast shower of pulverized rock. Huge chunks were torn away from the cliff face and thrown outward in every direction. On the left side of the canyon, the rocky knob that had been the target sheared away and slid downward, taking with it a half-dozen Comanche warriors. They fell almost six hundred feet to the canyon floor, twisting and tumbling through the air, arms and legs flailing, to land with sickening thuds on the rocks below.

To the right, more of the same. Three warriors cartwheeled outward and downward, their weapons flying from their fingers.

Suddenly, all of the noise stopped. Warwick's men in the canyon ceased firing, and all along the tops of the ridges, not a sound was to be heard. The white smoke from the two cannon and the rifles drifted upward on the thermals. Somewhere in the distance, beyond the canyon walls, a prairie dog barked, but that was all. The silence hung over the canyon like a blanket.

White Eagle, glasses to his eyes, watched the smoke rising from the rocks on the canyon floor. Thirty soldiers, no more. Where were the rest of them? What were they doing?

Again, he was startled when Yellow Crow nudged him with his elbow and pointed. He lowered his glasses a little, turned his head to see what he was pointing at, but could see nothing through the heavy pall of smoke that lay in the canyon. But then, he saw something.... Two huge puffs of smoke followed a second later by two thunderous bangs that echoed and reverberated off the canyon walls. There was a wild shriek and then two deafening explosions on the cliff faces just below the natural breastworks behind which his men were under cover.

White Eagle watched in awe. It seemed as if the mountains were crumbling. Great cracks and rifts appeared in the rocks, giant sections of the clifftops parted and slid downward, taking several of his warriors with them. What had happened, he had no way of knowing. Now, all was quiet. His warriors, and the blue coats on the canyon floor, had all ceased firing. Silence had descended over the mountains.

His face pale under the black war paint, he looked sideways at Yellow Crow. The man's face was a mask, his mouth was open, his eyes wide, as he stared down into the canyon at the broken bodies of the warriors far below.

For once, White Eagle was at a loss. He had heard of the big guns, but never had seen one, let alone seen one in action. Now there were two of them, here, and....

For a moment, he stood, head down, staring at the clouds of smoke rising over the mouth of the canyon, deep in thought. Then he seemed to gather himself, slapped Yellow Crow's arm, stepped forward, raised his arms, shouted to his warriors, and then pointed to mouth of the canyon. Almost instantly from every ridgetop, his men opened a hail of rifle fire and arrows on the two stands of bushes behind which the two guns were hidden.

"Ah, so there you are." O'Sullivan spotted White Eagle at the far end of the ridge on the right side, waving his arms and shouting something he couldn't hear.

229

The silence that had descended over the gorge didn't last for more than a couple of minutes.

"Reload, Mr. Morg–"

He was interrupted by an explosion of rifle fire from the ridges. The junipers in front of Morgan's guns were torn to shreds by a hail of Minnie balls. The air was filled with flying shards of wood, twigs, and branches. Morgan and his gun crews dropped to the ground, their hands over their heads in a vain attempt to ward off not only the storm of Minnie balls, but also the whirling spears of wood that were ripped from the trunks of the junipers.

The gunfire from the ridge didn't let up, even for a second. A sustained hail of lead steadily stripped away the cover from the two howitzers. Two of Morgan's men, still flat of the ground, suffered mortal wounds, and one to the neck, the other took a ball through the top of his skull. Three more were wounded, two of them severely.

The main column was out of sight and range, but O'Sullivan, Daly, and Coffin, some several yards to the rear of the cannon, fought to stay on their horses. They wheeled, reared and kicked as the concentrated hail of lead droned in on them, and hundreds of arrows fell from the sky.

"PULL 'EM BACK, CAPTAIN. GET THOSE BLOODY GUNS OUT OF THERE."

O'Sullivan and his two companions wheeled their horses and galloped the fifty-plus yards back along the wadi to where Lieutenant Whitworth, at the head of the column, was waiting. They dismounted and handed the horses off to a trooper who took them away to the rear. A few moments later, Morgan and what was left of his crews followed, dragging the two big guns behind them.

"Lieutenant Whitworth, Sergeant Major Coffin, Mr. Daly, have the men dismount an' move forward to the mouth of the canyon an' see if you can drive 'em off the ridges. I don't think you can, but we need time to relocate the howitzers. Mr. Morgan, you're with me."

Together, O'Sullivan and Morgan watched as more than a 150 troopers moved into positions just south of the mouth of the gorge and began to open fire at the Comanche on the ridges. O'Sullivan had been right. The hail of fire his men threw up had little effect on the incoming fire. The enemy had the benefit of the high ground, and the cover the natural fortifications it provided.

"All right, Mr. Morgan. The only way we're gonna beat 'em is to batter those bloody ridges all to hell, an' we've gotta do it bloody quick. It will be dark soon an' they will get away if we don't. Bring up the guns an' place 'em hereabouts; there ain't much cover, but it's gotta be done. White Eagle is up there. I saw him just as they opened fire on you. That's where you need to concentrate your fire. Forget the right side, direct both guns on that corner section there, at the left side an' that section of the end wall." He pointed. "Don't wait for me. Get 'em in position an' open fire when you're ready, then keep firing, fast as you can. Don't stop until I give

231

you the word. Now, go to it, an' good shootin' to you, sir."

It took Morgan only a couple of minutes to bring his guns to bear. The minute they were in position, he opened fire with explosive shells. For a few seconds only, he watched the flight of the shells and took note of where they landed. Then he made two small adjustments of the elevating screws and aim, and turned his crews loose.

Morgan's men were battle-hardened veterans of the war, and among the best at what they did. To O'Sullivan, they were a thing of beauty, a well-oiled machine that, every twenty seconds, hurled their messengers of death and destruction skyward to slam, seconds later, into the cliff face.

Slowly, the ridges gave under the onslaught. Dozens of explosive shells tore into the top of the ridges. Great sections of rock and ridge sheered away. The defenders, those who didn't fall into the rift, were exposed to the rifles of the dismounted troopers.

White Eagle watched in horror as dozens of his warriors fell before the hail of cannon and rifle fire.

The rifle fire he knew he could withstand, indefinitely, but only if his fortifications remained intact. Without them, he knew it was only a matter of time, and how many of his people would die before the blue coat guns. He was no fool; he was beaten, and he knew it. He had to stop it. He had to get his people out of the caves and away to safety. He had to talk to the blue coat leader.

He looked around, spotted one of his warriors behind a large, nearby rock, firing arrow after arrow into the air. He ran over to him, tore the white shirt from his back, tied it to the barrel of his Spencer, then ran back and leaped up on top of a rock, and waved it in the air. The gunfire from the canyon floor slowed, then stopped altogether. A few moments later, four small figures walked out into the open; one of them was carrying a white flag.

They met at the center of the canyon floor, close to the great fire pit: O'Sullivan, Daly, and Coffin; White Eagle, Yellow Crow, and Broken Nose. The ridges, pathways, and caves were alive with Comanche warriors, women, and children, all watching.

"You win, Nantan Oh-sull-van. I not know you bring big guns. Take me. Let my people go free."

O'Sullivan heaved a great sigh of relief, then shook his head. "It is good, White Eagle that you no longer wish to fight a battle you cannot win. Many lives will be saved. But I cannot let your people go. You must come in with me, all of you, to the great Fort Larned to meet with General Sherman."

"No, Oh-sull-van. That cannot be. Only elders can decide this. I cannot. You must give me time. If it is to be, it must be done with honor. My people deserve this honor. If it is not to be," he said, sadly, "then we must fight again. I will leave women, children here; take warriors and go into mountains; fight until we die. No other way, Oh-sull-van." He stood very still, tall, proud, and waited for an answer.

"We can grab him, sir," Daly whispered in his ears.

White Eagle heard him, and smiled, then looked at his white flag.

"No, Lieutenant, we can't. He's under a white flag, an' so are we." For several moments O'Sullivan stood, deep in thought, then he shook his head. "This is not good, White Eagle. I understand, so I do, that honor is at stake, but my orders are specific: I am to bring you an' your chiefs to Fort Larned. If you come peaceably, your people will be relocated to lands in the eastern Colorado Territory. If not...." He left the alternative unspoken and stared at White Eagle.

"I will speak to the elders. If they agree, I will do as you ask. I, Yellow Crow, and Broken Nose will come with you. But you must give me time, Oh-sull-van."

"How much time do you need?"

"Two days. You let me and people leave. We," he waved his hand toward his two chiefs, "return sunset two days, here."

Coffin grabbed O'Sullivan and pulled him back a few feet. They stood with their backs to the Comanche and Coffin said, "Don't do it, Colonel. You cain't trust 'em, an' if they don't come back, you'll be high an' dry an' probably end up in the bloody stockade for your sins.

An' I'm talking not just about them, but about Carson, too."

"Carson, that boy's gonna get court marshalled when we get back, so he is. No, Boone. I have to let him talk to his people. That way we have a chance at a peaceful settlement. If not, we'll have to fight an' kill 'em all, every last one of 'em. Them was Sherman's orders, an' I cain't do that. I don't have such a thing in me. I have to give it a chance, have to." He turned and walked back to the waiting group. Coffin followed, looking decidedly ill at ease.

"White Eagle, before I let you do this, I must have your word that you will return... in two days, as you just said."

"I do not lie, white man. I give word. By time sun sets in two days, we meet again, here. You wait, I will come. White flag."

"Then there is only one more thing before we agree: you must turn over your captives - the Bryson family, and the other woman."

White Eagle nodded. "It will be as you ask." He turned to face Yellow Crow and said something to him that O'Sullivan could not understand. Yellow Crow was visibly upset. He did not speak English and had understood not a word of the preceding talk. He snarled something at White Eagle, who dropped his hand to the knife at has waist, and waited. For a long moment, Yellow Crow stared at him, then he nodded once, turned, and trotted off to the rear of the canyon.

"He go fetch Elva, Dora and children. He be back soon."

Five minutes later, the chief returned, dragging Elva by the arm, the Brysons trotted along behind them. He stopped beside White Eagle and, with a flip of his wrist, sent Elva spinning toward him.

White Eagle glared at Yellow Crow, then turned to Elva. "You go now. You, Dora, children, all go with blue coats. You safe now."

She looked up at him, unsure of herself, but he smiled at her, nodded, and gave her shoulder a gentle push in O'Sullivan's direction. Then he waved a hand at Dora, indicating that she, too, should join the soldiers.

"Two days, Oh-sull-van. I back here, before the sun has set, and we will talk again. Maybe peace - maybe war. Two days."

"Two days, White Eagle. I will be waiting."

Chapter 25

The Box Canyon, August 27

It was late in the afternoon; the two days were almost up. As they waited on the canyon floor, O'Sullivan and his officers were becoming more and more certain that White Eagle and his people would not return.

They were seated together on logs, O'Sullivan, Daly, Warwick, Whitworth and Coffin, around a small campfire set in the pit that had once been the Comanche ceremonial center. A contingent of twenty troopers were seated around a second campfire some twenty yards to their rear. They were to serve as O'Sullivan's escort during the meeting. Elva, Dora and her family had been given a tent and were with the rest of the command encamped to the rear, close to the mouth of the gorge. Pickets had been placed twenty-five feet apart all around the canyon. O'Sullivan had also placed lookouts up on the rim of the gorge, waiting for the Comanche to return.

The sun had just dipped below the mountains to the west when they appeared. The sky was still quite bright, light enough for them to make their way down the narrow pathways to the canyon floor.

It was not what O'Sullivan had expected. White Eagle was accompanied only by Broken Nose and a dozen warriors; they came under a white flag.

When they heard the call from one of the lookouts on the rim, the four officers and Coffin rose to their feet and waited.

"Greetings, Oh-sull-van," White Eagle said as he approached the group at the fire. "We are here. I keep my word." He was wearing his short headdress, but no war paint. He was armed only with a knife at his belt and his Spencer rifle, from which hung a piece of white cotton cloth. His companions were similarly dressed and armed.

"An' greetin's to you, too, White Eagle. Please, sit." O'Sullivan waved his hand to indicate the logs around the fire. The chief and Broken Nose stepped forward, over one of the logs and sat down upon it. The rest of the warriors stood in a semi-circle behind them. O'Sullivan waited until they were seated, and then he and his group sat and faced them across the small fire.

"I am puzzled, White Eagle. You come with so few of your people. Why? Where are the rest?"

"We have much to discuss, Oh-sull-van. I will tell you what the elders have decided, and then you must tell me if what they say is good."

"I will listen. Tell me." O'Sullivan nodded.

"The elders say there must be peace. That we will go to the lands across the mountains, and we will do as the blue coats ask. We will meet with blue coat general, and we will talk with him, but we will not go with you, Oh-sull-van. We will go with honor, in our own time."

"That, White Eagle, is unacceptable, so it is. You must come in with me, so says General Sherman. If not, then we must fight, and all of your people will die. This is not good, what the elders say. They must think again."

"They will not. We talked for one day and one night. It is decided. If you do not agree, yes, Nantan Oh-sull-van, we will fight. If you take me now, not honor white flag." He twitched the rifle and looked at the cotton rag. "Yellow Crow waits," he waved his free hand in the air and to the west, "in mountains. He will become chief of Kwahadi and he will fight to the death. Many Comanche, maybe all, will die; so will many blue coats. It is not good that you do not agree."

O'Sullivan looked at Daly, who shrugged his shoulders, but said nothing. Coffin, too, had nothing to say. He simply stared across the fire at the Comanche chief.

"Nantan Oh-sull-van. We will come to Fort as you ask, but not now. We come, thirty days from now; me, all Comanche people. You have word of White Eagle. White Eagle keep word. This you know. If this is not to be.... I will go, we will fight. What you say, Oh-sull-van?"

"Whewww." O'Sullivan let out a huge breath. He was frustrated, and for once in his long military career, he was unsure of himself. Sherman's orders had been specific, and seemed to be inflexible, but....

"You must give me a moment, White Eagle. I must talk with my people." He stood, his people also rose to

239

their feet. "We'll be back. Please wait." He walked a few yards to the rear, turned to face the campfire, and was joined by Daly and the others.

""All right," he began, "I can't make this decision without some input from you people. What do you think?"

"Christ, Colonel, we don't have a whole lot o' choice." Coffin, not normally so forthcoming, was obviously very worried. "We can fight 'em, an' we'll win, but at what cost? They ain't trapped in the canyon now. If we have to fight 'em, we'll have to chase 'em down an' we'll have to do it on their terms. They are masters of guerilla fightin'. We're lookin' at a runnin' fight across maybe hundreds of miles of unknown territory."

O'Sullivan nodded. "Mr. Daly?"

"I agree with the sergeant major, Colonel. We can beat 'em, but at what cost? You get it wrong, an'... well, God only knows what you'll face when, and if, we get back to Fort Larned."

"I ain't worried about me. It's the men I'm worried about. Holy Mother, there's been enough killin' over the last four years. I'm done with it, if I have a choice, so I am. Mr. Warwick?"

Warwick looked at him wide-eyed. "You want my opinion, Colonel?"

"Damned right I do. You'll be doin' the fightin', an' the dyin', so let me have it."

Warwick thought for a moment, then said, "Colonel, I have been with you for almost a year now. I know you, I trust you, and I'm willing to do whatever you think is right."

O'Sullivan grinned at him. "Hah, good answer, Mr. Warwick, good answer. All right, Lieutenant, let's hear what you have to say."

Lieutenant Whitworth gulped, hesitated then said, "What he said, sir, Lieutenant Warwick."

"Well said, Lieutenant. All right then. Here's what we'll do...."

They returned to the campfire and sat down.

"Here's the way it must be, White Eagle. You say thirty days. No! That is too long. Twenty days, White Eagle. Twenty days an' you have a deal."

White Eagle stared at him, then turned to Broken Nose and said something to him that O'Sullivan didn't understand. Broken Nose replied, waving his hands, but it seemed that White Eagle was adamant, and he finally nodded his head in agreement.

"Twenty days, then, Oh-sull-van. I will come to great fort with all people. I will meet with great general and we will talk."

"This is good, White Eagle. I will trust you to keep your word. If you don't... then many, many soldiers will hunt you down. That will not be good. I will wait for you at Fort Larned. By noon, when the sun is high in the sky, on Saturday, September 16th." He held out his hand to the chief. White Eagle looked at it, then at O'Sullivan. O'Sullivan smiled, "It's the way we seal an agreement; we shake hands; that way both know that it is agreed."

"White Eagle nodded his head, his face serious, and he slowly reached out and took O'Sullivan's hand, and shook it vigorously. Then he grinned widely and nodded his head to Broken Nose, who stuck out his hand. And then they were all shaking hands, O'Sullivan, Daly, the other three, and all of White Eagle's warriors, who were excitedly chattering away to each other.

Chapter 26

Fort Larned, September 10

The journey back to Fort Larned took almost fourteen days; they arrived late in the afternoon of September 10th. General Sherman wasn't there. He was away at Fort Zarah, but was expected back within the next couple of days. O'Sullivan stood the command down, had Captain Carson confined to his quarters, under guard, and turned Elva and the Bryson family over to the medical staff, such as it was. He was assured that they would be well looked after and would be provided with housing at the fort. All that being done, he spent the next couple of days resting and relaxing in his own quarters. General Sherman arrived back at the fort on the morning of September 12th, and immediately sent for O'Sullivan.

When he entered Sherman's office, he found that the general was not alone.

Captain Carson was seated in front of the general's desk, and he was smiling.

"Welcome back, Colonel," the general said. "I understand that the savage is still at large. I would like to hear your explanation."

"I'll be happy to give you one, General, so I will, but first I must ask what Captain Carson is doing here. I left him under house arrest, for insubordination, among other things."

"So I hear," Colonel," he said, dryly. "Captain Carson is here because I sent for him. If you would feel more comfortable, I can have him wait in the orderly office until you are through with your explanation."

"That I would, sir. I would like to discuss him with you when we're done with White Eagle."

"Go wait in the outer office, Captain. We'll talk when Colonel O'Sullivan is done with his report."

Carson rose to his feet, favored O'Sullivan with a grim smile, and then left the general's office, closing the door behind him.

"Now then Colonel. Sit down and please proceed, and it had better what I want to hear."

For the next hour, O'Sullivan described the events of the past five weeks and the outcome of his meeting with White Eagle. Sherman questioned him at length, and he questioned many of his decisions. He was also very unhappy that O'Sullivan had decided to leave the Comanche at large, and made it very clear that he did not trust the "savage," and did not expect him to keep his word.

"He will indeed keep it, General. I trust him. He did not need to return to talk with me, but he did. He kept his word then, an' he will keep it now. They will be here by noon on the 16th, I'll bet my life on it."

"You already did, Colonel, at least you bet your career. If that savage doesn't come when he said he will, I'll bust you back down to private."

"That won't be necessary, General. He will come in."

"He'd better. Now. How about his prisoners?"

"They are in good hands, here at the fort, General. All are in good health and unharmed."

"All right." Sherman locked eyes with O'Sullivan and said, quietly, "Now let's talk about Captain Carson. What the hell happened out there?"

"We were two weeks out, General, deep in the mountains. The scouts had found two trails with signs that a great many ponies had passed along both. I made the decision to split the command. I took the westernmost trail and followed the sign. Captain Carson followed the northeasterly route. I gave him direct and specific orders that, should he find the enemy, he was not to engage them. Instead, he was to send word to me, an' I would join him and a decision would be made when I did.

"From the reports I received from several of his senior NCOs, he found 'em all right. He found White Eagle's village an' thought it abandoned, on'y it wasn't. It was a bloody trap, so it was, an' in his eagerness to get revenge, he fell for it. They were waitin' for him, us. Up in the hills around the village, an' he charged right in. He lost nearly half his command, includin' Lieutenant Keogh, an' I cain't even begin to describe what happened to that poor bugger, how he died. Shouldn't have happened. Him and thirty-seven more, all dead, an' all because o' that crazy son of a bitch in the next room.

245

"General, Captain Carson is personally responsible for the deaths of thirty-eight of my men. I want him court marshalled and dismissed from the army."

"It's not going to happen, Colonel. He maintains he was merely carrying out orders, my orders."

"General Sherman, Carson disobeyed *my* direct order and, I repeat, thirty-eight men died because of it. He has to be disciplined, if it's only you bustin' him back to lieutenant."

"CAPTAIN CARSON!"

The door opened and Carson stuck his head in. "Yes, General?"

"Come in, Captain. Stand to attention, sir." Sherman glared up at him. "I've just listened to Colonel O'Sullivan's version of what happened to your command. It's much the same as yours, but you forgot to mention that he gave you a direct order not to engage the enemy. What do you have to say for yourself, Captain?"

"General, your orders were to take White Eagle or to kill him. I was simply carrying out those orders. I considered your orders to supersede those of the Colonel."

"Nonsense, Captain. That's not what they taught you at the Point, and that's not why you did it anyway. You well know that the orders of a commander in the field supersede any that might have been given on a prior occasion. You disobeyed the direct order of your commanding officer, and you did so for personal reasons.

You know it, Colonel O'Sullivan knows it, and I know it. Thirty-eight good men died because of you. By God I should have you court marshalled and busted out of the army, and I would, too, if I didn't need experienced officers.

"Captain Carson, you are hereby demoted to first lieutenant and your record will reflect your insubordination. And, sir, there will be no more of it; no more insubordination. In future, you will carry out orders without question. One more slip up, Lieutenant, and the hell with you. I'll have you busted out and jailed. Now get out of here."

Carson saluted Sherman, spun on his heel, cast O'Sullivan a withering look, and marched out of the office.

"Satisfied, Colonel? His career is ruined."

"No, not really, General, but it's better than if he got clean away with it. Those thirty-eight poor bastards we left up in the mountains have no careers at all."

Sherman, his eyes narrowed, looked hard at him. "I hope, Colonel, that this will be the end of it. For now, we wait. And God help you if White Eagle does not keep his word. That will be all, Colonel."

Chapter 27

O'Sullivan rose early on Saturday morning. Nothing had been heard of the Comanche chief since they had parted twenty days ago in the mountains, and he was worried, unable to sleep.

He sat at breakfast that morning with Lieutenant Daly and Sergeant Major Coffin. Of Carson there was no word. He seemed to have disappeared.

"So, we wait, an' we wait. Bloody frustratin', so it is."

"He'll come." Coffin sounded more optimistic than he felt. "He's dead if he don't. Sherman will wipe him out."

"Yeah, an' me too, I shouldn't wonder.... What's it like to be civilian these days, do you think, Mr. Daly?"

"Hahaha, you'll never know, Colonel, you'll never know."

And so it went on; they sat together, the three of them, drinking cup after cup of strong coffee, making idle conversation about nothing in particular. O'Sullivan checked the time every ten minutes, or so.

It was just after eleven o'clock that morning when the six-man patrol came galloping in through the gates. The lieutenant in charge brought his mount to a skidding stop outside the command office, leaped from the saddle, ran up the steps, and through the door. He

248

reemerged several moments later, ran across the parade to O'Sullivan's office, knocked on the door, and walked straight in without waiting to be asked.

"General Sherman asks that you join him in his office, Colonel. They are coming, a whole passel of 'em, 'bout an hour out. Should be here by noon."

"Good. Tell the general I'll be there as soon as possible. Please ask Corporal Haig to come in as you leave, an' thank you, Lieutenant."

"You need me, Colonel?"

"I do, Corporal. Go find Lieutenant Daly an' Sergeant Major Coffin. Tell 'em to hightail it over here as quick as they can, an' that they are to dress smart."

He scribbled something on a piece of paper, rose from his desk, went to the closet and withdrew his dress uniform jacket. He looked it over, nodded, satisfied, then slipped it on and buttoned it to the collar. No sooner had he fastened the last button, than Coffin and Daly burst in through the door.

"They're comin' by God," O'Sullivan was excited. "He kept his bloody word, so he did. I have to go meet with the general. You two stay here 'till I send for you."

He walked quickly out of the office, across the parade ground, up the steps and into the command office where he found General Sherman along with Colonel Leavenworth and several other officers talking together.

"Come in, Colonel." Sherman smiled at him. "Seems as the savage has kept his word, saved your skin."

249

He turned again and continued his conversation, "As I was saying gentlemen, I want only the chief and his council inside the compound. The rest will be corralled beyond the gates, at least for now. Have a guard drawn up inside the gates; two ranks. We'll wait for them there."

They stood together on the command office porch and watched as the men assembled, two ranks on horseback, facing each other, ten yards between them.

He's givin' him an honor guard, by God. That ain't like him; not at all. O'Sullivan watched from the steps as the Comanche approached. White Eagle, his chiefs, and the elders were all mounted on ponies. The rest of the band followed behind, their possessions loaded onto travois.

As they approached the gates, twenty soldiers on foot, all armed with rifles, ran out and placed themselves between the leaders and the main band. There they stood, weapons at the ready, and waited. White Eagle glanced behind him, saw what was happening, shook his head slightly, but continued on through the gates. Yellow Crow, Broken Nose and four elders of the tribe followed him.

Slowly, between the two ranks of mounted soldiers, the seven Comanche advanced until they stood together in front of the command office and the assembled officers thereon.

White Eagle looked up at them, "I wish to speak with General Sherman."

"Arrest these... these... savages, Captain," Sherman growled to one of his officers. "Disarm them take their horses and put them in irons. Do it now."

"WHAT?" O'Sullivan shouted. "You can't do that, General. I gave him my word."

White Eagle looked at O'Sullivan, tilted his head slightly to one side, and gave him tight, wry smile.

The captain yelled an order and two dozen armed men ran around from the rear of the office and surrounded the Comanche. Within seconds, all seven of them were down from their ponies, and standing before the officers, their hands secured in front of them.

"Your word, Colonel? Your word to a savage means nothing; nothing. And, by God, I can do what the hell I please, and you'd better keep your mouth shut.

"Lock these six up, Captain, and have this one," he waved his hand at White Eagle, "brought to my office. Inside, gentlemen, now; you, too, Colonel O'Sullivan."

The officers, including O'Sullivan, stood at the rear of the office; Sherman was seated behind his desk, puffing a huge cigar. White Eagle stood in front of the desk facing him, his hands tied together in front of him.

"White Eagle. As far as your people are concerned, I will keep the Colonel's word to you. They will be sent north into the eastern part of Colorado Territory where they will be given land, along with the Cheyenne and Arapaho. There, they must live in peace. If they do, all will be well. If not... well....

"Your chiefs and elders will stay here in the stockade until I can have them transported to somewhere safe, where they can do no more harm. You... you will stand trial for the murder of thirty-eight United States soldiers, and if you are found guilty, you will be hanged."

"My God, General. You can't do that." O'Sullivan was beside himself with rage; his face livid. "The man came in voluntarily. An' by God, those soldiers would still be alive if it weren't for that maniac, Carson, whom you saw fit to let by with no more'n a slap in the face. Goddamn it, Gen–"

"Enough, Colonel," Sherman shouted. "One more outburst and I will have you thrown out of here. What happened to those soldiers is for a military tribunal to decide.

"White Eagle, you could have abandoned your village, left it. Instead you chose to turn it into a trap, and you killed thirty-five soldiers and tortured to death three more. You're a goddamn savage and you will stand trial."

"And I ask you, General," White Eagle said. Would you abandon your home if attacked? No, you would not. Your troops made war on Comanche. War bad thing; men die. My warriors die, my children, women, die at hands of your blue coats.

"I have talked to many peoples since I talked with Nantan Oh-sull-van. I know what you did, Sher-man, in your war with gray coats. You call me savage; hah." He turned and looked at O'Sullivan. "You honorable man,

Oh-sull-van. This," he twitched his head toward Sherman, "this man has no honor; even your people say so. I expected no less from him. I came here only because I gave word to you, and to save my people. If I must die, so be it. I say no more." He turned his head back toward Sherman, hawked deep in throat, and spat onto the middle of his desk.

"Get that son of a bitch out of here," Sherman snarled. "Lock him up."

An hour later, when the ruckus was over, the Comanche beyond the gate settled, and White Eagle was locked safely in his cell. O'Sullivan walked purposefully across the parade ground, ran up the steps to the command office, flung the door open, and then barged straight into Sherman's office without knocking. The general was still seated behind his desk amid clouds of aromatic smoke.

"Why don't you come in, Colonel?" he said, sarcastically.

"That, General," O'Sullivan slammed an envelope down on the desk in front of him, "is my resignation. You can shove it, so you can. I've had it with the army." And he turned to leave.

"Not so fast, Colonel," Sherman said, quietly.

O'Sullivan stopped in mid-stride and turned back toward him.

Sherman picked up the envelope, and, never taking his eyes from O'Sullivan's face, slowly and deliberately tore it into little pieces.

"It's not quite as easy as that, Colonel," he said with a chuckle. "When you accepted your commission as captain in the regular army – just a few months ago, wasn't it? You also signed on for five more years. Resignation *not* accepted, Colonel. You're going to Wyoming. Seems we're having a little trouble up there, with the Cheyenne."

The End

Historical Note:

While this story is a work of pure fiction it is, in part, loosely based on one particular historical fact, namely the Massacre at Sand Creek. This was the spark that set off more than ten years of Indian wars that continued on and off for more than twenty-five years, culminating in the massacre at Wounded Knee.

White Eagle and his band of Kwahadi Comanche never existed. Nor did Captain Carson and Lieutenant Keogh, although there's no doubt that there were officers in the U.S. Army just like them. Nor did any of the members of Companies K and G. Colonels Chivington and Wynkoop certainly did exist, and their exploits are well documented.

Chivington did indeed lead a large force of Militia Cavalry and carry out the massacre at Sand Creek in November 1864. It was estimated that between 70–200 peaceful Indians, Cheyenne and Arapaho, two-thirds of them women and children, were killed and mutilated by his troops. It was also reported at the time that Chivington's men "took scalps and other body parts as battle trophies," including human fetuses and male and female genitalia.

It is also part of the official record that Chivington said, "Damn any man who sympathizes with Indians. I have come to kill Indians, and believe it is right and honorable to use any means under God's heaven to kill Indians. Kill and scalp all, big and little; nits make lice."

Colonel Edward Wynkoop was assigned by the Joint Committee on the Conduct of the War to investigate Chivington and the Sand Creek incident. The investigation did not go well for Chivington, and the committee condemned him and his soldiers "in the strongest possible terms." However, no criminal charges were ever brought against them, although Chivington's political aspirations all came to naught, because of the bad publicity that followed him for the rest of his days. He died from cancer in 1894.

Colonel Wynkoop served as an officer in the First Colorado Volunteer Cavalry during the American Civil War, and rose to the rank of major of volunteers; he received the brevet rank of lieutenant colonel in May 1865. During his time as post commander at Fort Lyon, Colorado in 1864, he tried desperately to bring peace to the Cheyenne, but was transferred in November 1864 to Fort Riley, Kansas. He was there during the Sand Creek massacre. Later, on behalf of the U.S. Army, he was charged with investigation of Colonel Chivington's conduct at Sand Creek. His findings led to Chivington's condemnation.

In 1866, Wynkoop became an Indian agent for the Southern Cheyenne and Arapaho. He resigned in December 1868 in protest of the destruction of Black Kettle's village in the Battle of Washita River. He later became warden of the New Mexico penitentiary and died in Santa Fe on September 11, 1891.

Thank you purchasing this book. I hope you enjoyed reading it as much as I did writing it.

If you did like it, I really would appreciate it if you would take just a minute write a brief review on Amazon (just a sentence will do). It really does help. If you have comments or questions, you can contact me by email at blair@blairhoward.com, and you can visit my website http://www.blairhoward.com to view my blog, and for a complete list of my books.

So, if you did like Comanche, you may also enjoy my other three novels of the Civil War:

The Chase

A Novel of the American Civil War

During the last few days of the Civil War, a company of Confederate raiders rode into the small Kansas town of Elbow. There they raped, pillaged and murdered among the local populace, thus triggering a chain of events and a chase that extended for more than a thousand miles across the grasslands and mountains of Kansas and the deserts of New Mexico.

Along the way, Confederate Lieutenant Jesse Quintana, a ruthless, cold-blooded killer without a conscience, and his men massacred a band of Comanche women and children. They fought two battles with Comanche War Chief, White Eagle, and murdered and plundered their way southwest along the Santa Fe Trail.

Quintana had a nine-day start over his pursuers, Captain Ignatius O'Sullivan and Sergeant Major Boone Coffin, along with an Osage Indian scout and a small company of Federal cavalry. The climactic end to the chase came among the mountains on the Mexican border six weeks after it began.

You will remember O'Sullivan and Coffin from the author's previous novel, The Mule Soldiers. Their adventures continue.

You can grab your copy on Amazon. It's free to read for Kindle Unlimited members. Here's the actual link: http://www.amazon.com/dp/B00V0VZ8ZK

Chickamauga
A Novel of the American Civil War

Just after first light on the morning of September 18, 1863, in the deep woods on the banks of Chickamauga Creek, a single brigade of Federal infantry stumbled into a full division of Confederate cavalry. So began one of the bloodiest conflicts of the American Civil War.

Chickamauga is the true story—fictionalized—of that momentous conflict. For two days, the Confederate Army of Tennessee, under the command of General Braxton Bragg, and the Federal Army of the Cumberland led by Major General William Rosecrans, tore at one another during a battle that ebbed and flowed, favoring first one side and then the other. But, the Devil is in the details, and a single, inaccurate battlefield report led to a glorious Confederate charge and the total and devastating defeat of the Federal army. Chickamauga is the story of heroism, desperate deeds, and death and destruction on a scale that had never been seen before.

The story of the Battle of Chickamauga is told through the eyes of the generals who planned the grand strategies, and the soldiers who fought, often hand-to-hand, one of the bloodiest conflicts in American History.

Chickamauga is the intense story of the young men—the everyday soldiers, who must fight, not only the enemy, but also their own fears and inner doubts to find the courage to face seemingly insurmountable odds. It's also the story of their superior officers, and the generals who control their fates—men who are determined to charge into Hell itself to achieve victory. You'll stand side-by-side with them as they contest one disordered, ear-splitting, ground-shaking battle after another.

The author weaves unbelievable, but true, tales of breakdowns in communication, insubordinate commanders, and strategies that falter and fail in the heat of total war. You'll learn of the iron bonds forged between friends and companions on the battlefield, and morals and ideals brought into question. You will become a part of a victory achieved through pure grit and dogged determination, split-second decisions, and total dedication to the cause. Chickamauga is the story of ordinary people in extraordinary times.

This 1863 battle—on the banks of Chickamauga Creek, the River of Death—cost the armies of both sides more than 37,000 casualties; it was the bloodiest two days of the entire Civil War.

You can grab your copy on Amazon. It's free to read for Kindle Unlimited members. Here's the actual link: http://www.amazon.com/dp/B00MBU78HK

The Mule Soldiers
A Novel of the American Civil War

On a balmy day in April 1863, Union Colonel Abel D. Streight, at the head of a brigade of Federal infantry, set out on a 220-mile ride to destroy the Western and Atlantic Railroad at Rome, Georgia. The most fascinating thing about the raid is that Streight's brigade of four infantry regiments, almost 1,800 soldiers, was mounted on mules, a huge problem in itself; few of his men had ever ridden a horse, let alone a mule. But not only did Streight have almost 1,600 stubborn and wily animals to contend with, he soon found himself being relentlessly pursued by the inimitable Confederate cavalry commander, General Nathan Bedford Forrest.

The raid soon turned into a running battle between Streight's raiders and Forrest's cavalry. For Streight, it was a long and tortuous journey across Northern Alabama. For Forrest, it was one defeat after another at the hands of the very "able" Abel Streight, even though he, Forrest, had the advantage of home territory and the sympathy and aid of the local populace.

There are some wildly hilarious moments involving the mules and their new masters; or is it the other way around? There's plenty of action and suspense, and an unforgettable cast of characters, real and fictional, animal and human; some you will come to love, some... not so much.

Streight's Raid took place at the same time as, and was loosely coordinated with, the more famous Grierson's Raid (the inspiration for the book, The Horse Soldiers by Harold Sinclair, and the movie of the same name starring John Wayne and William Holden). Although Streight was probably unaware of Grierson's Raid, it's certainly true that he caused a diversion that contributed to the success of Grierson's Raid, and much confusion among the Confederate pursuers of both raids.

They say that truth is stranger than fiction. This amazing story proves the point, for the end of the story is... well, unbelievable.

The Mule Soldiers is the true story – fictionalized – of Colonel Abel Streight's Raid into Northern Alabama that took place from 19 April to 3 May 1863. It is an enthralling and bittersweet story that will stay with you long after you have you have finished reading it.

You can grab your copy here on Amazon for just $3.99. It's free to read for Kindle Unlimited members. Here's the actual link: http://www.amazon.com/dp/B00R0AIA1O

CPSIA information can be obtained
at www.ICGtesting.com
Printed in the USA
FSHW020900130221
78600FS